THE LAST OF THE REAL SERIES PRESENTS:

BRETT KING

(Book 1)

MORIAH SHANDS

The Last Of The Real Series Presents: Brett King
by Moriah Shands Publishing Company.

Moriah Shands Publishing Company is an imprint of
Mitchell & Anderson Enterprises, LLC. Philadelphia, PA.

Cover design by: @CreativeBre Robinson

ISBN 978-1-54396-995-5

Library of Congress Cataloging-in-Publication Data is available upon
request.

For permissions contact:
MoriahShands@Gmail.com

This is a work of fiction. Names, characters, businesses, places, events,
locales, and incidents are either the products of the author's imagination or
used in a fictitious manner. Any resemblance to actual persons, living or
dead, or actual events is purely coincidental.

A note from the author…

When we got evicted from our crib in Willingboro, NJ we moved to West Philly. My family was doing bad. As the 2nd youngest of 5 at the time, I think I was the only one excited about the move. Coming to Philly meant Sunday dinner at my father's parents' house down North Philly (in a section known as Badlands), where I could hang with my best cousin, Asia, who helped me find my writers voice at age 10 (thanks girly). My internal hype was short-lived once my parents separated and Mom began to lose mental strength. I recall one-time Pops paid child support. Mom was feeling good this day so my brothers, sisters and I got $20 a piece! That hype was also short-lived when after some hours, Mom remembered one of the bills were due. She called us all in the kitchen and with a flushed red face, politely asked for the money back. I proudly showed her I hadn't spent my money yet and with a defeated smile she said: "Mommy's so sorry Baby Bop." That was something she would say a lot more over the years.

The look of defeat on her face that day in the kitchen still drives me. The tears she let fall quietly still drives me. That feeling of "we're not okay" at 7 years old. Still. Drives. Me. I had witnessed so much arguing, fighting, cops, DHS, dirty clothes, no food in the fridge, heating up the house with the oven and wearing coats to bed…straight poverty. Having to enroll in public school from being home-schooled was the hardest. I was the youngest in my class and had to fight EVERY DAY (new kid initiation I suppose). Pop-Pop (RIP) put me in karate and that's when I gained a fire nobody could oust.

Years later, I pushed myself to finish undergrad and was now living down Allegheny in North Philly. There, I was around everything I described in a poem I wrote back in 2014 called The Last Of The Real. A dying breed. Good people with cold hearts. They were the dream deferred's of the world. I had to tell a piece of their story if I could because we overcome by the words of our testimonies…

To those real ones out there who desperately want to make it out of a bad situation in life…I'm a witness that where you start doesn't HAVE to be where you finish. Money won't solve your problems. Not violence, endless sex partners, drug or alcohol abuse. Ignoring it is even more harmful! Facing the problem head on by discussing the issue and making a self-conscious decision to be better is the first step. Then? Become the change you want to see…

If one person reads this and decides to make a change—I've done my job. This series is going to change lives. Enjoy…
(P.S To my mom, Tonya, please skip the sex scenes! Lol!)

-Moriah S.

FAMILY HISTORY

It was cold and lonely in December of '92 on State Road for Allen Hill Jr. The air was different. Like death was hanging over his newfound home. One hour of daylight was more torturous than the 23 hours of darkness within the prison walls. The hustle never died within him so that's what kept the young man going. He was in for three years so far and still no appeal date for a murder-robbery charge. AJ was a man of power and he would not allow prison to break his mind. Even still, the truth was that he felt alone. He was constantly thinking of how that one night could have went down differently. It was eating him up every day so the anger continued to feel new and fresh. He just needed an appeal date. The prison guards respected him and some were on his payroll still, so he had some level of "freedom" but it just wasn't enough for him.

AJ wanted to be on the outside still handling business. Everyone knew him and his baby brother, Oliver King, as hood legends. The sons of Malcolm King. Every one of their soldiers followed their lead and ate well because of it. Together the brothers were a movement and even though they were feared by some and hated by many, they were revered as the best to ever do it in the drug game after their father. Especially where they were from.

AJ was the front man and Oliver, who went by Olly, was his right hand. Exactly two years a part, the two were often confused for twins, taking after their respective fathers who had many similar physical features. AJ was in charge because he was the oldest. Olly was smarter but played his role and got his money. He didn't want the power. He just wanted the money and respect. They were young guys, just 28 and 30 but they were running a tight ship in West Philadelphia! They were known to get money and severely punish anybody who got in their way. They had their section of the city on lock and if anybody wanted to move weight? They had to come through them.

1

AJ had just come back from his shower this day in particular and walked into his cell trying to think of more positive things—at least that's what he learned from Chapel. He saw that his beeper went off and called for his favorite guard so he could go make a phone call.

"Lil brother, talk to me," he spoke into the receiver.

"It's getting cold out here brother," Olly hesitated...

Olly had a decision to make. He talked it over with his wife the night before and she let him know he had to do what he had to do.

"Your brother is a dangerous guy, baby. Nobody cares about you in the streets and nobody is going to look out for you, the way that you are going to look out for you. I say just don't forget who helped you eat," Karen whispered in Olly's ear.

She was sitting on his lap in his study after he finished dividing up the last of his kilos to hand off to his crew. He would be out the game for good and would be able to do all the things he dreamed of. Olly was also looking forward to having some down time to peacefully read his favorite books without interruption. He was an avid reader. Malcolm X, Marcus Garvey, Martin Luther King and prolific poets like Langston Hughes, just to name a few, filled his bookshelves. Karen knew when Olly was in the study to leave him alone but tonight he asked her to hang with him so of course she said yes. It wasn't often that he spent a weeknight home.

Karen loved being with Olly in the confines of the mini mansion he built for them in Conshohocken. Everything was designed to Karen's standards. Marble floors to compliment all the French doors with gold handles. She hounded the architects until her master bed and bath that had a hot tub and stand in shower were built to perfection. A state-of-the-art kitchen, dining room, and indoor half-court basketball gym for her boys weren't even her favorite parts. She liked to think that the home movie theater was her favorite—but then there was the garage floor she had Olly re-do to fit her new Benz and Porsche. She was going for the showroom floor affect she said.

They had a huge backyard with a built-in pool and sliding board. Olly even had an outdoor bar constructed for family events but Karen knew it was for his parties. Invite-only and exclusive to the local ballers and pimps who had just as much if not more money than Olly. He was a millionaire and didn't deal with anyone who wasn't on his level or higher. As soon as someone came in the house Karen had them searched from head to toe and made to leave their guns with security. Some guest paid security around $200 to keep their piece on them but after a party or two, the invitees would soon realize that these gatherings were to have a genuine good time. They may not have been right in their methods of obtaining wealth, according to Karen's mother-in-law Susan, but it was Olly's life and as wifey following the lead of her husband, Karen never overstepped.

Karen liked the life she lived, while Susan felt her son's wife was wrong for condoning his behavior. She felt her boys lived too gaudy but she never said a word. Just tried to guide them right and pray for them. Add that to the fact that she was sharing in the riches…How could she scold them?

Susan King started staying with Olly and his family after AJ got locked up. She said she was just helping Karen take care of her two grandsons, Brandon and Brett but in all honesty, they were the only family she had left. She lost many friends and family due to the drug game but couldn't seem to get away from it.

AJ's father Allen Hill Sr. was an abusive drunk who threatened to kill Susan and at the time her baby boy AJ, if she ever left. In the beginning of their love affair Susan still wanted to party from time to time with the local young people her age. Especially the players. That's how the pair met in the first place. Allen was a local gambler and drug dealer at a clubhouse in Baltimore on Pennsylvania Avenue. Susan was looking to be kept and Allen Sr. was in the business of keeping women. Things started out sweet and loving. A sinful bliss. Susan chose not to see the signs that were all around.

Eventually over time Allen Sr. became more controlling and more demanding, which eventually turned violent. They had many fights and she had countless black eyes to show for the bid she put in. After realizing how dysfunctional her family structure was, with the help of her sister, Susan fled to West Philly with AJ who was just one years old. That's when she met Olly's father, Malcolm King. Susan had a type for sure. He favored Allen Sr. in many ways on the outside but on the inside Malcolm was refined like pure gold and she saw him as her savior.

Big Malc was all that. He was a fair skinned guy with fuzzy brown hair that he wore cut low. His face was covered with freckles and he had this smile that she just couldn't resist. He was a very charismatic guy who was selling heroin all over the city and was loved by many. Malc fell hard for Susan and began to love AJ like he was one of his own. AJ grew up believing Malc to be his biological father for many years.

By the time AJ was 13 Malc was sentenced to life in prison for his drug trafficking and because he started off by selling drugs down south, he was sent back to his home state of Alabama to serve his time. He admonished his sons to stay out of the street. All of that didn't deter AJ though. He still wanted to be down. He wanted to be his own man like he watched Malc do. He wanted to get money like the local pimps.

AJ held off on the street life for a while but after seeing his favorite play cousin get shot and killed by a rivalry gang, AJ grew cold and turned to the streets.

3

Susan was always depressed and drank away the money that Malc managed to hide. A young Olly soon realized that he was going to have to get money on his own and that wasn't going to happen unless he started selling with his older brother. He thought his big brother was too hot headed because he was always fighting—his women, workers and rival gangs. AJ was a leader though. Olly wanted to lead as well but in his own way. He envisioned helping his community. He understood that selling dope was temporary until he met his goal. He promised himself that when it was time to stop, he would. Olly didn't see selling drugs as a life-long plan and that day had come quicker than he thought. The brothers were just built different. Olly and AJ were the good and the bad.

"Enough has to be enough for you one day, Daddy," Karen whispered, bringing him back to their conversation.

He sat back and looked at his 23-year-old queen. She was a pretty fair-skinned girl with long sandy brown hair and deep brown eyes. For having just had a healthy baby boy named Brandon five years back and now Brett who was just born that past August, she still kept her body tight unlike some of the girls he knew who had kids. Karen was beautiful and Olly couldn't get enough of her. He wished they had a little girl but he was more than satisfied with his two sons.

Karen was petit in height and build—she was only 5'2" and 130 pounds—but her personality made up for it. She had a laugh and smile that could light up any room. She really kept the ship rolling when he was out making moves and doing his thing. Olly had other chicks on the side but Karen wasn't worried about that. She had his heart and that's all that mattered.

Olly knew Karen didn't believe him but once he made up his mind that he would marry her, he put his player cards down and focused on his family and his empire. Too often groupie chicks got in the way of his focus. Karen helped him smarten up and start seeing the bigger picture. Besides, Karen was his biggest supporter and believed in his dreams of being a music mogul.

Olly owned a bar on Girard Avenue, where he had a hot female DJ on the turn tables for lady's night. Karen and her girls would stop past but other than that, she stayed out of his way. Olly was young and she wanted him to live it up while he could. He was immature in some ways and even with two kids he still stayed in the streets. She wanted him to stop but didn't press him. Some called her crazy for being a down ass chick, but she didn't care. They were happy and they were in love. Olly had to admit that he was liking his new family man lifestyle. Karen gave Olly a breath of fresh air and made him consider changing his ways.

"Yeah you right, Baby. I've definitely had enough. I can't play this game forever. I'm going to just let AJ know what I'm up to, put his half in the safe and then I'm done. I let all my dogs know. They already

4

started making their own crews. I can't keep fighting. I got you and the boys to think about now. It's like what can I do at this point?

"People ain't going to understand that this move is bigger than me. I got my first two artist and we ready to hit NYC with some big-time producers, Baby. We are going to leave this city and never come back," he said trying to convince himself.

Olly knew AJ wasn't going to just let him go without a fight but he had to try to make a better life for him and his family. He had enough saved to start his businesses and some life savings. Olly and AJ had touched their first million together. After acquiring more than enough in his eyes, Olly was now content with what he had. He managed to stash money in a few different locations throughout Montgomery County for Karen and the boys if anything were to happen to him. He knew it was only a matter of time before the Feds came knocking on his door...

"Ain't nothing colder than in here," AJ stated, snapping Olly back to reality. "I heard that mixtape you put out with your new group Geed-Up. They real good. I been selling them by the case," AJ laughed.

Yeah, he shouldn't have been selling his brothers mixtape without giving him a profit but after all he was the one in need of some money, right?

"Thanks man I appreciate that, ha. But seriously though we gotta talk business. I'm coming up there Saturday to kick it to you," Olly responded.

AJ knew his baby brother better than he knew himself and he could feel the distance in his voice. "You can tell me whatever you need to tell me brother, I'm talking on a secure line," AJ stated.

"This is some face to face kind of shit. I'll be up there Saturday," Olly pressed.

"Little brother, don't make me get upset, okay? Just tell me what's up so Saturday can be a chill visit," he demanded. Being locked up for 5 years so far and missing out on his nephews being born was beginning to take a toll on his patience.

"AJ..." Olly sighed. Then he said it.

"It's over brother."

"Hahaha! What's over? I hope you not talking about my business. That's never over baby boy. We in this for life. You know my lawyer is trying to get my time cut down with parole. So, the way I see it, I'll be out in no time," AJ tried to argue.

"Brother...we're done. It's not the same out here without you and—"

"Alright, alright..." AJ interrupted.

At first, he was happy to see that his brother paged him but now he was furious and his mind wandered back to that hot Florida night...

AJ got caught up after robbing the connect. He put in the time and now wanted to be the connect. The brothers already had a deal with Old Man Jules. An older Dominican gentleman who lived in Miami. Olly felt Jules was good to them and wanted no parts of the plan. AJ wanted to make his own mafia and was recruiting any young brother willing to make a few extra dollars, showed loyalty, and were willing to move all this product! AJ made his usual trip to Miami to re-up when him and one of Jules security guards shot and killed the old man in his mansion in a quiet cul de sac in Coral Gables. Jules whistled for his fight dog to attack AJ before he took his last breath. The dog tore into AJ's left ankle—ripping flesh—leaving him with a permanent limp.

AJ wasn't pushing the weight for more than a week when the Philadelphia district attorney, Eric Jefferson, got a tip from a Miami PD lieutenant that AJ was the one who killed Jules. No one knew how or when. But after successfully getting Malcolm a few years prior, they were trying to get AJ as well and this was all the ammo they needed. The DA only had one witness at a local convenience store and one in Jules neighborhood. The first witness said they saw a bleeding AJ run inside, grab a few first aid kits, throw a hundred dollars at the cashier, then run out before grabbing his change. The old beat up security camera they managed to use as evidence was nothing but fuzzy looking shapes moving on the television screen. After drawing up a sketch and comparing it with Jules neighbors account of what happened, who said they heard the normally quiet fight dog bark hysterically, the prosecutor was looking to pin the killing on AJ and take down the Jules Cartel at the same time.

The DA tried his best to get Olly indicted as well but nothing would stick. He was…clean. No priors, not even a suspension in high school. To be the brother of AJ Hill and the son of Malcolm King, attorney Jefferson just knew it had to be some dirt on him. He tried getting help from an old kingpin friend of his named Jeffrey McCoy but the McCoy's wouldn't help in any way. Trying not to lose his cool, Jefferson knew one brother was better than none and focused on convicting the notorious AJ "King" Hill, Philly's most recent menace to society.

With AJ locked up and Jules dead, things started drying up and on top of lawyer fees, Olly knew it was only a matter of time before he would have to start using his savings to keep things afloat. The streets didn't come with a retirement plan or pension.

Once Karen got pregnant with their youngest son, Brett, she begged her man to straighten up and leave the streets alone. Brett was such a happy baby born on what felt like the hottest day in August of '92. Full of spunk and laughs. Olly had a soft spot for Brett that he didn't have for his oldest son Brandon and that's when he realized it was time to get out the game.

6

This motherfucker thinks this is a game. Not a problem. If he leaves me in here to rot while he goes and makes millions without me then he has the wrong idea, AJ thought to himself. He wished Olly would have come with him to take out Jules. Olly was smart and would have made sure everything ran smoothly. AJ was starting to grow bitter and began blaming Olly for his seemingly dark fate.

"Listen brother—I know it's looking dead right now and you got your dreams of selling records, but I still see life. I'm in here making flowers bloom out of concrete in the winter time baby boy! You still eating cause I'm hungry!" AJ yelled as the guard came back in letting him know his time was up on the secured line.

"Allen…I'll always be your brother but I'm on to different things now," Olly stated. Jules was dead and with the feds waiting for one screw up—Olly did his last bit of rounds in the city he made his riches from and that was the end of an era.

"Gotta go. Oh—and it better be my full half waiting for me. Don't worry I'm getting out of here," AJ huffed.

"I'll be in touch AJ," Olly solemnly promised.

"Sins of the father carry down to the next generation brother. Just remember that, aiight?"

Olly was left with the dial tone and an eerie feeling that that wasn't the last time he would have to deal with AJ.

ONE

Present Day
May 2015

S he started off by saying she wasn't feeling the kid. Honestly, I
thought she was lying from the start. Better yet, I knew she was.
The only thing that had me partially believing her was the fact that she
wasn't giving up the yams. No cheeks for weeks. That's what the
homies would say. First her number wasn't saved and then she moved
up to 'No Cheeks.' I mean to be quite frank bitches always fell through
for me. Before you get mad I refer to some females as bitches because
that's all they are and they refer to themselves as such. If you're a lady
then you'll always be that to me. But like I said, they would always
slide…but not this one. I didn't know what it was but she wasn't with
the shits.

Either she had somebody or I, Brett King, was friend-zoned. It
all started with a DM. She hacked her cute homegirl Charmaine's
account saying she was new to Snapchat and to add her so you know I
did! She kept avoiding me so I sent one last DM.

Me: Why you always fleeing me? I'm just trying to get to know you.
No Cheeks: You got a lot of swag and I think you're cool. I see you one
of them hood corporate dudes and you gotta be young as hell. Baby
face ass nigga. I respect that, but I'm chilling.

Girls just be confusing for no reason. Like, damn am I getting
the ass or not? I gave her my number and told her if she ever wanted to
talk to hit me up. Do y'all know it took this girl three fucking weeks?!
THREE! I don't know what was worse. Her taking so long to respond
or me counting. Probably me counting.

I finally got the text when this shorty named Maya that I call
Uptown asked me to take her on a date to the movie tavern out King
of Prussia. I knew her since undergrad and we always blew it down
while studying for Mr. Brownsen's management class. Never slid up in
her cause she had a fiancé at the time and I wasn't trying to break up

what looked like a happy home. The whole date was filled with silent laughs and texts between me and No Cheeks. Uptown was irritated of course but what could she say? It was me.

"I mean, if you want to come through you can. Come through and roll me the fuck up then fuck me nigga," Uptown laughed trying to take my attention off my phone.

Behind the laughs I knew she was serious. Once her and the bul broke off their engagement, she always wanted me around. I fucked with her but she was too pressed sometimes. She knew how I was living and she wanted to be my trophy. But I ain't see her that way. Just as a good time. Uptown knew that and said she was cool with it. I still kept her at a distance because girls go crazy when they think they have potential to change a nigga. You can't change a man and that's just the actual factuals.

Now mind you, the whole time I'm getting the yams from Uptown I'm thinking about No Cheeks and how she stopped texting me back after I told her I was still out around 1am. The blunt that me and Uptown smoked had me paranoid, like maybe—just maybe—No Cheeks knew what I was up to. Then I thought *What did she know?* I finished busting Uptown down and tiredly let her spend the night. I just ain't feel like taking her home…

When I got into work the next day, I found out I was getting a promotion at my job and would be acting as the hiring/training manager. My boss had six candidates in mind and I was mandated to hire one of them as an understudy to take on my old spot by the end of the week. I liked working by myself and wasn't ready to play babysitter for some newcomer. It was easier and if anything went wrong I would be the only one to blame, you know? So far, all these interviews were with some corny dudes. All of them were qualified but you got to have some type of swag rolling with me. I was flying all over the world and I couldn't have anyone messing up what I started so far.

Later that week I was at the crib checking my work email. Right before I got to open one of the final resumes, my youngin' started clownin' me.

"B-Boy! I follow that jawn Charmaine. She 24 but I can bag her! Char a fine ass redbone and she friends with No Cheeks. Char like Gina and No Cheeks is like Pam. Call me Big Marty Mar cause I'm bagging both of 'em since you playin'," he laughed.

At just 19 years old Shook used to be a great running back before he dropped out of high school. We were working on his GED but he only wanted to do music and was letting me manage his upcoming rap career. He was getting some local buzz so things were looking good. I made sure I always kept him around me so I could keep him out of trouble. I had invested too much time and money for it all to get messed up over some street shit.

"You still ain't hit that chocolate bitch?" Jay asked dickeating.

10

Jay was Shook's 1st cousin. I was the only one who didn't fuck with him 'cause he was too joe, but Shook insisted he was good people.

"It's plenty more hoes in the hood but damn B-Boy—you missed out on that one," Shawn said laughing and counting his money.

Shawn was a good friend that was more like a cousin. He used to work with me at my Uncle AJ's tire-shop back in the day. Apparently Unc and Shawn's fine ass mama Ms. Layla had a thing back in the day and ever since? Unc always looked out for Shawn like he was his own.

"Man, fuck these hoes and get this money. Wassup with this game of Spades though? $100 and ten points per book. Don't get all ya books? Pay the fuck up. Y'all know how we do it. I got Brett, fuck y'all," D said shuffling.

Delando, aka D, was my old head. Shit he was everybody's old head and what he said was law. Everybody else knew him as Big D but he was just D to us. I met him at a local summer league like five years prior and we ended up coaching together. To top it off we won the prize money. We talked business at every practice until we started tossing ideas off of each other. I guess you can say that's when we became business partners. He was helping me manage Shook's appearances as well as setting up our lounge. D had a family to get back to so he never stayed out any later than three in the morning or Dina would start tripping. That's his long-time girlfriend and the mother of his two sons, David and Daniel, who were my godsons. Off rip, D let everyone know that he ain't play about his girl and the kids. He was like a hood ass Dr. Huxtable. Anybody that gave Dina problems already knew D was going to end it so for the most part everybody stayed clear.

After D gave the Spades arrangements out, Shook was mad he couldn't join in but sat and watched anyway. Shawn and Jay started crying saying D and myself pull in the most bread out of the group, and how it wasn't fair that we were always on the same team. D yelled for my Blue-nosed Pitbull named Blue and said:

"Blue! Uncle D got some bitches for you!" Blue came running and barking making Jay hop up. We all laughed as we passed the blunt around.

Jay had his lean and Shawn would take a few sips but I was cool off all that. It was what we did every Thursday night at my crib on Greene Street in the Germantown section of North Philly.

As always, me and D was killing these niggas. I did renege twice making D storm off yelling something about how he should've teamed up with Shawn. I blamed it on the fact that I had too many shots. I mean I did have too many shots but I never fucked up in a game of Spade's. Me and D *were* eating like kings compared to them. On the other hand, they barley had enough to pay their bills and child support sometimes but it never failed, they always had their Spade's money ready. Jay was jobless and Shawn was always buying expensive bikes. Unc tried to help him budget but the man was addicted.

We were running a little organization and all managed to not get caught by the pigs except for my brother Brandon. Uncle AJ taught us everything we knew about the game since we were young bucks and always told us to have a cover up. On paper we were all law-abiding citizens with good employment. I went to school for marketing and worked at New Enterprises, D was running his own construction company and Shawn was running Unc's tire shop now. 9-5 during the day and then after that? We sold little shit like weed and percs. I would arrange a cocaine deal through a friend from undergrad every now and then but for the most part we laid low. It didn't pay much at first but since my older brother Brandon got locked up we weren't splitting everything up like before. Jay and Shook didn't know about our little operation and that's the way I wanted to keep it. Like I said, I didn't really fuck with the bul Jay like that and Shook was my artist. I didn't need them knowing all my moves.

Uptown: Beard Gang want some company?
Me: For sure
Uptown: Well me and my girls coming through. Ima bring Tee for Jay corny ass, tell em we said hennything is possible lol

Got the text and so it was on as it always was. Me or Shawn always had the bitches coming through and they were always down for whatever. We were selective though and they knew our one and only rule. Bring a bottle of something top-shelf and we all good. Not no personal jawn either. The big boy so we can have some fun.

The next day was a Friday and I forgot I had another round of people to interview—just two—but after Spades and entertaining the ladies I forgot to look over their resumes.

I pulled out my copper colored slip on loafers, some money green tapered cut slacks, and a crisp short sleeved white button-down shirt. I decided to toss on my gold crucifix chain that Unc gave me when I graduated from college. Greased up my low cut—making sure my waves were shining—combed my beard out and ate a bowl of cereal since I was running late.

"Lockup when you dickheads leave!" I yelled to Shook and his girl from the previous night. Shook was crashing at my place for a while. I figured it would be better for business and for Shook. He was a wild bul when I caught him battling other rappers for dollars at the summer league. I offered him a way to get seen and he took it. He was the little brother I never had.

I got in my blacked-out Lexus truck and headed to work. I knew Lincoln Drive would have heavy traffic so I decided to put some music on from Shook's mixtape and got comfortable. I loved Fridays baby!

"Good morning Ms. Mary. You looking good today girl," I said with a wink as I gave her a surprise cup of coffee from her favorite shop down the street. She emptied out her office brew and smiled.

"Thanks baby. I was with your mom last night and we so happened to be riding by your place. We saw all of them fast girls going in there. Is that why you're late today?" She was always being nosy.

"You tell Ma I said stop taking you to the bar and to mind her business," I said jokingly.

As I walked down the hall to my office Ms. Mary followed behind me, letting me know my first interview was with her niece who just finished grad school. She said she got her Master's degree and had been looking for work in the marketing field for a while. She assumed I would think she was cute. Ms. Mary was always trying to hook me up with somebody. I told her I don't date my current or future coworkers which made her laugh and go back to her desk. I didn't even bother to look at the resume. I just took a deep breath, said a prayer that this would be the last person I had to interview and opened my office door.

"Damn." Black Jesus moved quick.

No Cheeks was sitting there on the waiting room couch with her headphones in. She was fixing her lipstick in her phone screen. She didn't even realize I was standing there watching her.

"Man," I whispered to myself.

This girl was even sexier in person. A sloppy but perfect bun topped her head like a crown against her smooth chocolate skin. She had on a black pencil skirt matched with a tight, shear baby blue blouse and some black leather stilettos. Just sexy enough to show her curves and yet still professional. Little mama was peanut butter thick. Her light brown almond shaped eyes were covered by gold rimmed glasses that gave her a sexy nerd look. By their thickness I could tell she couldn't see for shit, ha. Shorty was clean and she was just the person I was looking for.

"Welcome to New Enterprises. Would you like a glass of water?" I asked trying to keep my cool.

No Cheeks hurried to put her phone and headphones in her purse, grabbed her folder, and declined the offer, as I led her into my office. You would have thought she didn't know who I was.

As I went through all the formalities of the interview I noticed she knew everything about the company for the most part. When it got started, who started it and even offered what we could do to expand our reach. She was thorough and very detailed just like her aunt, Ms. Mary. She showed some good business ethics when I threw a few client privacy questions her way. I liked her style. I just had to make sure I wasn't thinking with my dick and making a good business decision.

This would be my first hire/training and I had to make sure this was the right choice.

"Well Ms. Simone Grear," I said glancing at my notes one more time.

"Mr. King?"

"You'll definitely be hearing back from us soon."

"Do you have a timeframe?" She pressed.

"Uh...should be no more than 2 weeks. We have a few more candidates to consider," I stated. I noticed she sank back into her seat and I found it amusing.

Since she wanted to be petty and keep calling me Mr. King like she didn't know me, I figured I'd leave her in her thoughts. My guy, baby girl had the job once I saw her in the waiting room! Not to mention her MBA that sealed the deal. No Cheeks qualified for a better position but you needed tenure with the company to get them. We only hired for some positions from within the organization which she was well aware of. She was a woman with a plan and I could respect that. All in all, I had to maintain my cool.

"Thank you very much for your time. I'll be looking forward to hearing from you," she said with a wink as we were saying good bye.

She left out so fast I didn't even have time to ask her what she was doing for lunch! She still hadn't responded to any of my text or Snaps. Shit she didn't even open them! Shorty was playing hard to get and I think we both knew this new position was the perfect way to get her.

TWO

The following week I decided to let Simone know the good news. I wasn't sure I was ready for what I believed would be a rollercoaster ride but I was excited to have her on my team.

"Oh my God! Kiiing! Thank you so much for this! This really means so much to me. You just made my day!" Simone squealed. *I guess I can't call her No Cheeks anymore, huh? Or can I?* I thought to myself smiling.

"Well I'm glad I could do that for you. We start Monday. Now I know it's already Thursday afternoon, but tomorrow is when all the execs turn up together at happy hour. You aren't obligated to come because you wouldn't be getting paid for your time, but you would be meeting the important people at New E.N.T in a chill environment. I really want you to meet one of the best in the business—Ms. Shayla. To top it off it's open bar on the company's dime thanks to your new boss, Jon, AKA China Man." *Please just say yes…*

"I will be there." She responded. *Bet!*

Later that night, I hung out at this open mic spot I helped manage from time to time for D's little uncle, Khalil, on Baltimore Avenue. Khalil lived on the same block in the same house his whole life. When his mom passed, he inherited the property and turned it into a three-story pool house/open mic joint he named Lil's House. He knew me and D were trying to run our own spot eventually so he let us manage his for the experience. Plus, he knew wasn't nobody gonna get it poppin' like us. I loved working for Khalil because he was our age, always let us drink for free and I could use the spot anytime for whatever. As long as he got his renters fee of two stacks, we were all good. It was closed this night in particular for maintenance so I was there to let the contractors in. I decided to look over some work for a client, made myself a whiskey on the rocks and figured I would text Simone. I know I technically just hired her but I had to stay consistent, right?

Me: Hey Ms. Simone

Simone: LL Cool K

Me: LL huh? What you up to?

Simone: Ladies Love Cool King…Corny I know lol. I'm watchin ratchet TV.

Me: Nah I like that lol…oh no not them girls

Simone: Gotta get my laughs in

Me: I hope u ain't like that

Simone: And what is it to u?

Me: I need some class on my team

Simone: I popped out classy baby boy. Thanks for today, it means everything. I've been looking for a job for a while now. You're a life saver.

Me: I'm glad I could do that for you, my treat to dinner? To celebrate.

That was it! At that point I was ready to say fuck it and keep it strictly professional.

"I ain't pressed over no bitch not texting me back," I said half drunk and frustrated. I hit the jawn Tee's jack, blew it down with her and got some crazy sloppy in the back office. I ain't care that she was Uptown's friend because she was always down for a good time and wouldn't ask no questions or nag. I talked with Tee for a few after I took her home, sold her a quarter of sour and then I headed home myself.

***

'If we don't get this paper who the fuck gon' get it?
It's money to be made, my nigga, no time for quitting'

My 6AM alarm was Shook's very first mixtape intro. It was motivational and I always had to have it in my mind 1st thing in the morning that money was to be made. The only thing that comes to a sleeper is a dream, you hear me?

I did my daily workout in my basement. I ain't no heavy weight or nothing but I could bench press a little something, usually 130, then I would run on the treadmill for a half hour. I made myself a glass of orange juice, an egg white omelet with peppers, onions and cheese, and some beef bacon.

After showering, I decided on a 3-piece navy-blue suit I bought from my suit maker out Houston. Oldhead was sick! Just tell him what you want and he'd ship your clothes to wherever you were. I cuffed the pants, paired it with a white crew neck shirt and some white loafers that were collecting dust in the closet. I wore the vest open and left the jacket home since it was too hot for all that. Just a simple summer time lay. Stylish and breathable in this heat but still corporate.

16

I fed Blue, let him out back where he chilled all day until I got home, and I was out. It was a pretty normal morning.

"Mr. King? You have a call on line 2," came Ms. Mary's voice on the intercom.

"Thanks Ms. Mary…This is King," I said taking the call.

"Dog wassup!"

"Who's speaking?" I asked. Nobody in the gang besides D had my personal line.

"You don't know your own brother now? I know them rich boys ain't fuck up ya memory too." *Brandon!*

"Bro! My bad dog, I'm used to accepting the call first. What you got a cell in there?" I laughed.

"Yeah well Mom came through on her word and got her sexy lawyer friend to help me out. I'll be out in a week. I'm on her cell right now. I'm going to be staying at the spot." The spot was his longtime on and off again girlfriend Tina's crib. The one who helped some niggas set him up and thrown in jail the first time. At least that's what the streets was saying.

"My nigga is back, huh," I smiled.

"You know it!" Brandon replied.

My brother was coming home and just in time for the summer. It was unreal. Mom's connections ran deep throughout the city and right when it was looking dark Mom came through, like always.

"Okay, I'm looking at my calendar now. I got a business meet up that day and then I was heading to the open mic me and D running. You know *Lil's*. You might as well come through. I can grab us a table. I can move the meeting and come pick you up," I suggested. "We working on opening our own spot called D&K's Lounge. It's still under construction right now though," I continued.

"Oh, that jawn. What about the strip club? I need to be around some bitches when I break out," He said uninterested. Brandon didn't vibe with D and jail didn't change that one bit. They were both the same age, 28, and butted heads all the time. The one thing they had in common was their love of the chase of getting more money. He felt like D took his place in my life. Brandon got locked up off and on since I was 12. He would come home for a few months or a couple years and then he was locked up again. Nobody could ever take my brothers place though and I didn't feel that I had to prove that to anybody—especially Brandon.

This last time Brandon got locked up was on some killing shit that they didn't really have no evidence on. Or at least that's what we paid his lawyer to make it seem like. Brandon was still running with some dumbass bitches that·Uncle AJ said stay away from. The chicks were cool with Tesson McCoy and all his folks. Tesson was one of the younger brothers of the notorious Spade McCoy. It was only a handful of cartel families left in the city and the McCoys were one of the only

17

ones still standing. There were a few others like the Williams', the Bigsby's and the Moore's. However, besides us Kings, the McCoys had always been seen as the biggest competition.

Now I don't compete with anyone but I guess the Kings and the McCoy's had beef back in the day so it was always a problem with them. Brandon was banging some of Tess nephew's chicks as a way to bother the McCoy's. Flipp, who was Tess nephew always had a chip on his shoulder when it came to us. So, Brandon hated Flipp and vice versa since high school. They found out they were both fucking the same bitch one night, a fight broke out at some bar around Unc way and Brandon drunk ass shot Flipp's youngbul supposedly in self-defense. Knowing Brandon, it was on purpose.

"The strip club, huh? Yeah that'll be cool too..." I said focusing my attention back on my spending report.

"Okay well a lot can happen in a week, you know? You keep running business as usual and we'll see what ya schedule looking like when I touch down. Plus, you know Tina prolly got something nice planned for me. It's been a while since she got some dick and I know she waiting, haha. Anyway, when I get there I got some things I wanna discuss," he stated.

We talked for a few more minutes before he told me he had to go. I told bul be safe and we hung up. My mind started racing. I already knew what he wanted to discuss. Fronting him some cash so he could get back on. Things were calm and we had no slip in the army of three. Me, D and Shawn were running a tight ship and with the help of my security connect Eddy, we were doing just fine. Brandon had a way of being seen and heard. I just wanted the money. My guys understood that and I knew they would have questions once I let them know he was coming home. Mainly because they were all loyal to me.

See, the guys respected Brandon simply because he was my brother and his uncle was thee AJ King. However, everyone had grew accustomed to the calm once Brandon got locked down. I was uneasy about giving up my peace in exchange for the storm he always brought with him. I forced myself to focus on the positive fact that regardless of what he wanted to talk about—he was breaking out that jail cell and was getting his murder charge dropped. I couldn't have asked for anything more...

RING! RING!

"Damn it's Friday why everybody calling, shit." I mumbled to myself around 2pm.

I was trying to chill, listen to my music and just finish my monthly report, but the phone was ringing all day. I also wanted to have something to show Simone for her Monday start date. Her training would be a crash course because we were set to hit France in August.

"This is King," I said not hiding my irritation.

18

"Hey Mr. King, this is Simone." Before I could get anything out she was right at me: "I have a dilemma. My ride for tonight is tripping on me and I would *not* ask for a ride like this but I really want to come along and meet everybody," she said sounding hesitant.

"Not a problem. Where do you want me to meet you at?"

"I'll text you my friends address now. Thank you so much."

"No problem." I said hanging up.

I didn't say yes 'cause I was about to get some alone time with shorty, even though I was, right? I honestly loved how eager she was to be around the business. I could tell she wanted to know the ends and outs and I was honestly happy to show her. Simone seemed very thorough and calculated and it intrigued me. Something I wasn't used to with the girls my age…

I left work a little early to meet up with Simone and I'm glad I did. I got some time in with her because of traffic and soon realized how much I liked being around her. She was quiet but not shy on the way to the bar. She was just chilling and comfortable—like she belonged there riding shotgun with me.

"So, you ready to meet the team?" I asked breaking up some silence during the radio commercials.

"Yeah I am. I can't lie I'm a little nervous but I'm ready," she said looking at me.

"No need to be nervous shorty, I got you."

"Oh, you got me, huh? Well thank you for having me," she laughed.

"You're very welcome. I hope you enjoy yourself. I think you'll fit in fine and I think having Shay around will be nice too. We're the only black people there besides Ms. Mary and Trevor is an Oreo so you know we gotta stick together," I joked.

In a way I was serious. The job could be cut throat at times and having some faces you could identify with felt good. We always had to be a step ahead and put our best foot forward.

"Okay, cool…" Simone responded sinking into the seat more.

I could tell she felt protected and that was a good sign. I could see myself getting used to her but stopped my mind from wandering.

Dina's was Dina's restaurant where she was the head chef and she always made sure the food was on point! It even had a little dance floor. D convinced her to flip her crazy cooking skills into money and helped get her spot opened. It was the hottest upcoming bar and grille in the city. My higher-ups asked me to hook them up with some happy hour deals we could vote on for first Fridays. Something about team building. I think they just wanted to get drunk on the company's tab. So, because of all the good press it was getting and with some of my convincing—*Dina's* was a unanimous decision. See, my coworkers may have worked in the city but they weren't from here so I knew they would trust my judgement. I always made sure the family ate.

"Stace! Some shots for everybody please," I asked Dina's friend from culinary school. We had been at the spot for about thirty minutes and I was ready for one of Stace's special shots. She always had some secret concoction ready for us. Had to have been the coolest white chick I knew and she could make any drink you wanted. She wanted to run her own bar one day and was working for Dina to get some experience during the week and planned to work at me and D's lounge on weekends.

"Oh no, haha, no shots for me. You can just give me a slushie with the house whiskey, please," Simone said, peeking from behind me.

Me and my old head Shayla started bidding. We always started off with shots! I already had two shots of the house whiskey that night with Trevor. He was celebrating a new baby girl and his oldest son just got accepted to an Ivy league college. We drank to everything. We worked hard during the week so we deserved it.

"Come on just one!" Shayla laughed.

Shayla was already half drunk and screaming *"do it for the sistah's!"* Simone was finally down for the round of shots that eventually turned into three.

I introduced her to the team of execs. Seven in total. Jim, Trevor, Shayla, Nancy, Tom, Miguel and Bill. At the base of things—I don't want to bore you guys—we acted as liaisons for big companies all over the globe as product managers. The France trip coming up? Fashion line shit. Tokyo? A start up smart watch company that could customize any watch you wanted to connect to your phone and TV. Some accounts had lots of money and some were just starting out. The goal was to score big accounts, make everybody look good and move up. I was the new guy getting started even though I was doing it for 3 years already. I started as an intern and landed a permanent role after graduation. I was working on landing a big account but mainly got stuck with quick start-ups. Once I saw the training job open up, I figured I could get used to a steady check instead of commission. Right after applying I landed the France gig. It was an okay gig but this wasn't what I saw myself doing until retirement.

"Loosen up some, this is a chill thing. You not at work," I laughed to Simone who looked a little intimidated. I got a little closer to her and whispered, "now these motherfuckers got money. They making $200,000+ per account and who knows what kind of side hustles they got. Shit I'm making way less than that but eventually you get used to being in a room full of all this money," I reassured her.

"Yeah I haven't been to a business mixer in a long time. Once my shots kick in I'll be cool," she smiled back.

"You're lucky Baby Boy. I didn't get an assistant until just a year ago. And this one is cute!" Shayla said sipping a margarita at the end of the bar. She was watching me interact with Simone all night.

"Naw she ain't no assistant Shay, she taking my spot," I reminded Shay, who just nodded her head and grinned.

Shayla was like a cool ass old head that you always wanted around. Like the rich single aunt who brings gifts for everybody at the family holiday party, ha. She even kicked it with my mom a few times. Only thing was she knew me too well and I had to keep my composure around these guys. I was private and didn't need any insinuations about my business relationship with Simone. But damn she was fine! I couldn't help but to look at her. She had this powder pink halter dress on that was hugging her just enough to even make Shayla do a double take. She had on an expensive vintage looking good bracelet, gold hoops and some gold sandals. Mone was simple but very stylish.

Shayla could tell Simone still seemed a bit uneasy. I nodded my head to her and then back to Simone. Shay got the hint, grabbed Mone's hand and said:

"Let's dance girly, y'all young girls gotta help keep me looking young," she laughed. After that it was on…

"Ard y'all get home safe and somebody get Trevor's ass a fucking taxi!" Tom laughed.

I told Dina and Stace to be safe locking up as me and Simone walked everybody to the parking garage. Simone was feeling "too lit" (she didn't want to be that on) so we grabbed her the fries she kept asking for from a truck that was still out on Broad street and then made our way to her crib…

"Make a left at the light and then turn right. I'm at the end of the block. I really had a good time, thanks for the invite and for the ride," she said gathering her things.

"Your welcome, Mone."

I pulled up to a house on a quiet little block in Mt. Airy which was different from where I picked her up earlier that day.

"So, this is where Simone Grear stays?" I asked.

"With these ratchets? No fucking waaay. Like. Nah. This is my little twin sisters spot…I just spend the night sometimes. I don't like to though," she said zoning out for a second.

"Wait you have a twin?" I asked in shock.

"You wish. No silly, my little sisters are twins. I call 'em Twitches for fun," she said getting a good laugh out of her little joke.

"They think I act like I'm too good for them but I just have different goals and they don't listen to me since Mama…They just hating on me 'cause our lives ended up different. I still spend the night almost every Friday so I can see my niece and nephew. Maaan, I got this new gig too? What? A bitch is 'bout to be hurting they feelings for real now," she said shaking her head in sarcasm. I couldn't help but laugh. It was like I was watching her Snap. I didn't like that she called herself a bitch but I didn't pay it no mind.

21

I wanted to know more about her evil twin sisters and what happened to Mama…but I wasn't going to press. I knew she was a little drunk and just talking.

I parallel parked the car to my liking, leaned my seat back and asked:

"Why you got me dropping you off and picking you up from random spots?"

"What's it to ya?" She said with a side-eye.

"Well you know you put your home address as one thing on your resume and now…" I said stopping mid-sentence. I was feeling a little stalker-ish.

"Stranger danger!" she giggled leaning her head back and closing her eyes.

"Yeah, okay. I did have to interview you. Man whatever, ain't nobody stalking ya ass if that's what you thinking," I retorted.

"Wouldn't be the first time…I can't say it would bother me though," she shrugged.

"You be busy on Sunday's? I'm having some friends over and I would like to see you," I asked. Me and the fellas were planning a little cookout in two weeks to celebrate summer and Brandon's return and I had to have her there.

"You waste no time huh? Why you want me to come over? You wanna show me off?" She said smiling and rubbing her thighs.

Next thing I know she pulled me in for a kiss and I started rubbing her ass!

"This is why I don't like shots," she whispered stopping abruptly.

"Why 'cause you get loose?" I laughed.

Mone rocked back and forth ending up back in my face leaning across the seat, making her breast spill out her dress just a tad. She took her glasses off and started staring at me.

"Okay let me be serious…Since we're going to be working together let me get this out now. We both young. I just turned 26 and you're only, what? Twenty-two? Twenty-three? Yes. You cute and I know I'm sexy as hell…Look, I know you want me Brett. You a real thorough young nigga, you know?" she said in deep thought.

"But…I don't fuck my bosses," she continued.

"I turn 23 in August and I'm not asking to fuck. I just want you to come to my cookout at 2pm on Sunday in two weeks," I said with my hands up paired with a perfectly played shocked face.

"Oh…well whatever. Wait! I know what I'm trying to say and I know what you're up to. Like I said I don't fuck my bosses," she said wagging her drunken finger at me making us both laugh. *Busted.*

"So yes, you can look all you want and I shouldn't have just kissed you. Don't think you getting any of this cookie little boy," she laughed.

I sat there trying to calm my jimmy down and just smirked. More of a grimace than anything. She made me want her even more by this stupid ass game she was playing. So what I was young? I could handle whatever she threw my way. I just needed the chance.

"I love the way you look at me sometimes Boss Baby…that's not good," she stated.

"What you mean?" I asked innocently.

"I'll see you at work on Monday," she said rolling her eyes. I laughed as she got out the car. She lit her blunt, took a long puff of it and walked into the house through the side door without looking back.

"Damn," I said to myself frustrated. I could've killed the pussy right there in the car. At least that's how it always went. I wasn't worried though. I always got the girl.

THREE

B ro, what you mean you chillin? Since when?" Brandon said sternly.
It was a week later on a Saturday morning when we were finally
reunited.

"I'm just saying I got some ends now. Plus, I'm managing the
little bit of work with the guys...I'm not trying to mess that up." I
replied looking to my uncle for a life-line. Of course he didn't say
anything.

Uncle AJ decided to tag along and told me to keep my money.
His boy was home from jail so he was treating. We were having
breakfast at this spot called Mt. Airy's Finest Diner on Germantown
Avenue that Unc ran, and was in the process of owning. Everybody
came through to see the hype behind Finest. They also came to see if
they would catch Unc in the back cooking or if one of his celebrity
friends would be stopping through. No one knew the real behind Unc
or how he managed to still be on top even after getting locked down
for so many years. He took so much pride in Finest and was always
bragging about how his customers loved the diner's fresh coffee and
pancake platters. We sat in the back by the cooks so that we could talk
business just like old times.

"I'm just saying this time is different, Baby Boy. We talking
millions of dollars. With Unc's connect, my hustle, and your money talk?
We looking to get paid nigga! Unc got a better connect for us. He got a
chemist in the lab right now cooking up some new shit. We gonna be
paid fucking with the Chinks! You graduate college a year early and
don't want to use none of them smarts for ya own team. Just selfish.
Unc said it's a go so stop being pussy. You been hanging around D too
long. That old ass Lexus and that corny watch ain't gonna get ya new
assistant's panties, B-Boy," he joked making us all laugh.

"Ah whatever, nigga. She ain't a hoe so I gotta put a little more effort in that's all. All I'm saying is it's not the same out here man..." I said quietly. Brandon waved me off and started looking at his menu.

"How we gonna clean the bread?" I questioned.

"That's where you come in young blood. Look at your team, find the strengths and go from there. You gonna need more than one way though, so keep that in mind," Unc stated looking up from his menu.

Unc hadn't really been in the streets for years and had turned his life around but whatever his connect offered him must have been good enough for him to get back in the game. Everybody was trying to get paid. The plan was to start setting up some businesses to clean the money. I would have to get Eddy in on this or at least get his thoughts of how to push this new product undetected.

"My business potnah gonna break down all the logistics to us. He is guaranteeing we make a profit of 70% off the first shipment. Depending on how much it is will determine the payout. Anything after that is up to how deep we willing to go with this thing. I'm talking on ya way to A-list status so you can do what everybody put you through school for. Maybe that marketing shit will really work out for you this time," Unc said making Brandon laugh.

They both kept chatting for a few more minutes trying to talk me into doing the deal. I knew they were trying to get paid, but I learned over the years that dealing with these two was only guaranteeing me some type of trouble. The only one who was going to look out for me was me.

"Listen I hear y'all," I said winking at the waitress walking past.

"See Unc that's why he soft! He always running after bitches instead of focusing on his bread," Brandon said throwing sugar packets at me.

"I can't help that these niggas baby moms want me," I laughed.

"But seriously," Brandon continued, "you know we need you. You got the smarts that I need and I got the muscle that we need to flip this bread. Then we put the fellas on like always but slightly different. It'll be like Pops and Unc back in the day. They'll work for us and we'll be filthy rich," he said rubbing his hands together smiling.

I noticed Uncle AJ change his expression when Pops name was mentioned. Like he was agitated but covered it up by looking at the cook's work. It was like Unc tried to avoid any conversation about him at all times. Pops got killed right when Unc got out of jail when I was still in middle school. The murder was a cold case but I hoped one of these days the streets would talk.

"What about the youngbul that used to run for you?" I asked.

"Nah. He ain't never gonna stop selling loud. He content. Look nigga if it's 'no' just say no," Brandon said fed up.

"Just give me a few days to think—"

"A few days? Negro, time waits for no man. I need this decision ASAP. I'm driving to New York Monday afternoon. I'll give you 'til tomorrow night." Uncle AJ interjected.

That was the end of the discussion. Unc didn't really take anything but yes for an answer.

"Aight. Happy to be home?" I asked trying to ease the tension.

"Man, it feels good. I'm ready to make this money. Like the bitches coming through been cool. Blowing it down with my niggas been cool. Even seeing Moms and y'all been cool. But I'm ready to make this fucking money! I love it." Brandon was Philly's Money-Making Mitch. His hustle was like nobody else's but he wasn't the smartest so he made dumb decisions. He wanted to be a boss but was more of a worker. I knew that and Uncle AJ knew that but Unc had a soft spot for bul so he let him ride. Then you had Ma always saving B's ass.

"Look I understand you all corporate and shit now like Ma, but you know you tryna see more than the 215 and a few places you've visited with ya job. I know you don't want to just go to them fancy places for work. When the last time you went to Paris and turnt the fuck up? Don't worry. I'll wait," he said cracking up.

"Nigga shut the fuck up," I said laughing. This new weed he grabbed from somebody he was locked up with was crazy. I felt like I had an edible or something. We all ordered so much food and left a hefty ass tip for the cute waitress.

"My compliments to the fucking chef baby. Y'all ain't have to make my eggs that good." I said to her as we got up to leave.

"See Unc? He needs days to think about the money but seconds for these bitches, gotdamn! I should be sweating the hoes. I'm the one that just got home," Brandon snapped.

"You right you need to be getting some ass right now like ya big homie. I'll catch y'all later." Unc said sweet talking some chick on the phone. He got into his freshly detailed all black pick-up truck, honked the horn after busting a u-wee and then sped off.

"He really the smoothest old head I know. He really still out here getting this bread!" Brandon admired.

For the rest of the day we tried to catch up on some of the years that we missed out on. I brought Brandon to the barber shop and got him hooked up with a fresh cut. After that I took him clothes shopping and then we went to see some of the properties I wanted to own. The more I showed him these places the more appealing Unc and Brandon's offer sounded. I wanted to buy the city! For a youngin' like myself, $50k a year may sound like a lot but after student loan payments, taxes and other bills, I was honestly just maintaining.

My little side businesses were still in the startup phase so I wasn't really banking off of them yet. I was on a retainer for one of the real estate businesses I helped manage, but even still, I wanted to be wealthy. I wanted the fan-fare. I wanted the love and the hate. I wanted it all. Ma always said *"you can't have it all baby boy,"* but I wanted everything. She knew this and because she didn't want me involved in the streets she pushed me with the academics. Many said I had street and book smarts. I just figured I had some balance.

Me and Brandon were leaving this bar called Stripes right off of Broad and Cumberland. They had the best seafood platters and they were always generous with the drinks. Some of the bartenders who knew us from social media made sure we had a good time.

"Man, today was a good day. You doing ya thang baby boy," Brandon said rubbing my head as we walked to my car.

"Yeah I'm doing alright," I responded.

"No bullshit little bro. You making Pops proud," he said quietly.

Pops died in the summer of '03. I remembered that weekend like it just happened. We were all getting ready to go to New York for a day trip. Pops had some music shit to handle with a producer who was interested in his fourth try at managing an artist. A few before fizzled then died out but he felt this time around would be different. He said he had to make a stop by one of his homeboys cribs earlier that morning to drop something off but he never came back home. Mom was pissed and figured he was with some chick when she got a phone call. She looked like she saw a ghost or something and dropped to the kitchen floor.

"Not my Olly! Oh God not my man!" she screamed into the phone...

"...He always said you was different. You make a good hustla' but you a corporate dude for real. He always said you was going to take the clean road and do something with yourself." Brandon continued, snapping me back from my thoughts.

"Oh yeah?"

"GET DOWN!" he yelled.

A blue Impala pulled up at the light. Two dudes leaned out the front and back passenger windows and started firing rounds at us in the middle of Broad street.

We pulled our pistols out and started letting off a couple shots then ducked down behind a white van to avoid the rest of the bullets coming our way. It was too many bullets. People were running and screaming trying to find a place to hide. My whole life flashed before my eyes. My mom, my homies...Crazy enough—Simone came to mind...I also prayed to God that he got us out of this one alive. The sound of sirens was getting closer making the Impala speed off down Venango. I sat there for a second. I was stuck.

"Get up Baby Boy! We gotta go nigga!" Brandon hollered.

27

We ran across the street, hopped in my car and sped off in the opposite direction. The rest of the ride to Tina's up the Northeast was quiet. I dropped Brandon off and the whole ride back to my crib I thought about grabbing a new piece to add to the collection. I had a lot of thinking to do. Like was really going to do business with Brandon and Unc after what just happened?

FOUR

K ing? Are you okay?" Simone asked with concern. It was first thing
Monday morning and Simone was excited to be at work. Her
attitude lifted the whole office atmosphere and she was trying her best
to help lift my mood.

"Oh yeah, yeah I'm fine. Now, when you create the excel sheet
make sure you name the report. It seems like something small but
you'll be surprised how overlooked that is," I continued. I was looking
in my phone at the news report to see if anybody was talking about the
shooting. So far, no suspects and of course there were no witnesses.

I told Brandon and Unc I was in. Now I know what y'all
probably thinking. How can I be so stupid, right? Honestly these two
guys were the only real family I had left. My cousins had been killed,
doing life or doing 15 to 20-year bids. So, when my brother comes to
me asking, practically begging, for help? I had to come through. I didn't
plan to be in it forever. I was going to work with them long enough to
flip some money and buy my buildings then be done with selling for
good.

"Hey kids," Shayla said as she stopped in my office.

"Wassup Shay. How was your weekend?" I asked.

"Y'all know Trevor?" She whispered.

"Not old ass Trevor!" Simone gasped.

"Yasss honey! Sheeet, that man has a baby leg ya hear me?"
she laughed doing a real clean twerk.

"Well damn Shay Shay," I said trying to get a better angle.

"Oh, Brett shut up and keep ya eyes on Simone," she grinned
making Simone roll her eyes and try to hide a smile.

If Shayla wasn't such a cool ass old head I would try to get at
her. By the way her and Simone were discussing this important news, I
could tell they were going to be good business partners as well as
friends.

29

"Ladies I don't want to picture Trevor naked," I interjected when Shayla started sharing details. That only made them giggle even more.

Right then I got a call from Unc. I let them share they're weekend stories as I walked out my office to take the call in the lobby.

"Check it out young buck, like I said everything is a go. You got a flight to catch real early Wednesday morning to meet the plug in Beijing. You'll be back here Friday night. You gonna be in and out. The time difference gonna have you tired, but you'll be fine. I'll have a driver take you to the airport. Get some Chinese pussy for me," he laughed.

"This is too last minute to get the whole week off. It's Monday Unc."

"Man, you told me you never take off. Tell 'em it's a family emergency or something," he suggested.

"In Beijing?" I responded more quietly.

"Look ain't that why you got a secretary? I ain't gonna be able to make it because you know they not letting me or Brandon's black asses into no fuckin' China. So, it has to be you, Mr. No Record. Brandon don't know I'm sending you. I got him laying low for right now with his probation and everything. If he asks you—it's for ya job. He can find out everything in more detail another time, aight?" he admonished.

"This is just last minute Unc," I said again.

"Talk to ya boss for the days and send the bitch in ya stead for whatever else and be ready for ya flight. Don't fuck this meeting up or it's ya ass nigga." *Click.*

I knew I would be able to get the rest of the week. My boss Jon was in a good mood and ever since I locked in my first and final big France account with his old friend Edward, I noticed he was more lenient with me.

"Take as much time as you need and let me know if you need anything else, sorry to hear that," Jon responded when I told him I would be taking care of my sick uncle for the week. I started thinking about what was so important that I had to take a last-minute trip to China?

Simone decided to join me this day for lunch and I can't lie—I was hype. She was like a break away from reality. She was quiet but was the perfect company. We were sitting out on the lunch deck. While she was crushing her burger and fries and laughing at a video on the Gram, I was barely drinking my iced tea and didn't really touch my chicken caesar salad.

"You busy Friday?" I asked already knowing the answer.

"What's happening Friday? You cool?" she asked noting my irritation.

"Ehh. I got something I may need to handle so I'll be out this week. Would you be able to cover for me at the weekly meeting?" I asked.

"Being as though I'm shadowing you, I think you need to either tell me I'm filling in or let me know if I may be filling in. Either way I'm going to be there." She answered not looking up from her phone. She had this brown skirt and a cream-colored sleeveless blouse on. She had some gold sandals on and her hair was out and curly. And them glasses. Man, they did it to me every time.

"Yeah…well I need you to fill in for me. I'll be out on some business. If you need anything just report to Shayla. It's only going to be Wednesday through Friday," I stated.

"Are you sure you're okay though?" She asked genuinely concerned.

No. No I'm not. My brother and Uncle kind of dragged me back into the game. I almost got shot on Saturday. My mom thinks we're just catching up on old times. Not to mention I want you to make it nasty for me and then go grab dinner and do it all over again.

But instead I replied: "just some family bullshit and the France trip. You excited about it?" I asked trying to look normal.

"Yes, I am! August will be here before we know it. I'm trying to buy something for my niece and nephew. I have never been outside of this country and I am ready—got my passport and everything," she smiled.

"You're smile is beautiful," I blurted out.

"I know…and I thank you for noticing. If you need to talk about what's bothering you, you got all my numbers. See you in a few. By the way I already started that report. You can give it to me all at once. No need to go easy just because it's my first day as your beautiful trainee," she winked as she cleared her trash off the table. *Damn, she tryna have a nigga in love*, I thought letting what she said linger in the air long after she was gone.

The rest of the day was really a breeze for me. Simone caught onto everything quickly. Ms. Mary kept coming to check on her which she let me know was driving her crazy. Simone was annoyed but she knew her aunt was proud so she let Ms. Mary be great. Simone was honestly ready for France. She still had to take the mandatory international business etiquette training but she was ready for sure. I had to pat myself on the back because this hire was a good idea…

"Have a good night Ms. Mary," I said as I locked my office and headed out the door the next day.

I waved to her as she talked to a client on the phone before getting on the elevator. Once in the main lobby I saw that the afternoon rain didn't let up. Simone and Shayla were standing at the door talking before Shayla's boyfriend pulled up.

"Like I said—fuck that nigga. We'll talk though and remember—don't worry. I'll see you tomorrow." Shayla said waving to me and giving Simone a squeeze on her arm.

"Hey everything cool?" I asked as I started to walk out the door. I noticed her ride in the tinted white car wasn't there. I figured she got stood up.

"Just waiting for the rain to lighten up some before I head home. I'm cool," she replied.

"If you want I can drive you home? I gotta stop by the crib first though so I can let my dog inside. I ain't even know it was going to rain."

She hesitated at first, then said: "Okay, cool."

On the ride home, I told her I would put in a request for her to get a temporary employee car. You had to be there at least a year to get one but I had connects and promised to pull some strings. Her laptop and phone were already ordered and, on their way, so getting a car would be the icing on the cake. I got out the car and let Blue in, checked my mail and ran back to the car. It was raining so hard and I was soaked so I took my shirt off when I got in the car. I caught her checking me out in my undershirt and I had to admit I was feeling like the man.

"Why are you so nice to me?" She asked as we made our way to her place.

"I'm gonna keep it a bean with you shorty. You a thorough lil' chick from the norf side," I said making her grin.

"No but seriously. This is a big transition working on my team and I want you to be comfortable. I was taught to always make a black woman feel safe. Make sure she's cool and to protect her no matter the bond." I said repeating what my father taught me.

"What about all the other women?" she probed.

"See, they have their men to protect them. I was taught to protect mines first. Malcolm X said that 'the most unprotected person in America is the black woman.' It's up to the stand-up guys to watch over them." Another lesson from Pops.

She sat quietly staring out the window just taking my words.

The rest of the ride was filled with traffic, jokes and singing along to the radio. I forgot I was only taking her home and I silently wished I had more time with her as I double parked on this small block in the Logan section of the city. Of course, we were at another one of her 'friends' house. She looked hesitant to get out the car and I rubbed her hand and said:

"You have a good night and I'll see you first thing in the—"

"Mone who the fuck is this nigga?" Some short stocky bul hollered walking up to my side of the truck.

She jumped out frantically and said: "Babe relax this is my boss. Chill! Brett thanks but you should go," she said running around the front to catch him. She looked terrified. I dated a girl once who had that same look in her eye when her ex ran up on us at a restaurant. I automatically knew this dude was beating on Mone and I got pissed.

Stocky Bul pushed Mone out the way and started banging on my window. Now, all I could think about was the fact that I wasn't at work and I was about to ball this clown the fuck up! It had been awhile since I had to put a nigga on his back. As soon as I got out the car I felt a hard jab to my lip. I started leaking all over my undershirt and I blacked out. All I could remember was Simone screaming and yelling: "Brett you're going to kill him!" I immediately stopped and stood back to see a whole crowd around me with Stocky Bul laying hunched over, moaning, and holding his jaw. You leak mines I'm leaking yours pussy—dress shoes and all! The rain let up a little bit and everybody had their phones out.

"Damn, that's the bul Brett."

"He got hands like his Pops!"

"She probably fucking bul and Travis found out."

"I know her pussy crazy they out here fighting in the rain!"

"Real shit. Trav look like a dickhead though fighting a King."

"Right! Trav get the fuck up! King a chill bul but ain't shit sweet about 'em!"

"Shit!" I whispered to myself as I heard everybody out there gossiping.

"Get the fuck in the house Simone. You really be testing me!" Travis yelled out.

Simone was sitting there looking hysterical. I told her grab her shit and come with me. She refused and started walking inside.

"Simone call me if you need me," I said as I pulled off. I felt so bad I decided to hit her up and apologize.

Me: Mone, I'm really sorry all this happened I didn't think the day would go like that
Simone: Yeah me either. Look thanks for everything.
Me: Don't be mad at me ard?

Just like that my response was green which let me know she blocked me for the night. I hated to think he was punching on her! I couldn't understand dudes like that. I tried to tell her to come with me, but you can't help someone who doesn't want to be helped, though. I wasn't into saving hoes. I did want to save Mone though. *Damn King…you got it bad for this one!*

FIVE

Thursday…Beijing, China

It was about 3pm local time when I pulled up to what appeared on the outside to be an abandoned warehouse sitting next to a sand dune in a desert.

"This is the best drug your people have ever seen. To answer your question yes—this is 90% pure. It is a new era and you will be compensated very well," Jose Ramirez said in a strong Mexican accent. He was Unc's connect and was doing business with the Chinks too.

"This is called Peak. Simply because at the peak of its growth it is most potent," an old Chinese man named Wang stated proudly. He looked like a stunt man from an old Bruce Lee flick. He motioned for his son to pass him the pill as he took his seat at the head of the table.

"This will cause money to flow through your hands in a manner that you have never seen before. I am sure of it. Be careful, trust your men, and never come up short when its pay day," Ramirez said with a smile....

Unc always comes through, I said to myself when I first landed at the Pudong Airport that morning. I thought I would have time to chill but these dudes weren't wasting any time.

I was met by two of Wangs men and driven to the Waldorf Astoria. I traveled to a lot of places before but I had never seen something so futuristic. It was big city living with all the drip to go with it. The whole city was just ahead of its time, literally. We were 12 hours ahead of the rest of the homies back in Philly. I had never seen anything like it before. It was the longest flight I ever took.

Around 1pm that afternoon my escort named Bo told me we were going to meet the two big men of the hour. Chen Wang and Jose Ramirez. Unc never mentioned I was meeting either one. They were in charge of running the biggest Mexican-Chinese drug cartel and the Alphabet Boys couldn't stop them.

34

As I looked at the tall skyscrapers and caught the dim sunlight trying to peak through, I couldn't help but feel like all my dreams were about to take off with this new *investment*, as I liked to call it.

The further out we drove, Bo and his partner said they were closing the partitions and windows in the backseat of the jeep we were in. I didn't even know a jeep could do that. A screen appeared in front of me on the back of the partition and some music videos started playing. I was starting to feel more anxious but I was bugging out with all this high-tech living.

When we finally arrived after hours of driving, the partition rolled down and we were in the middle of a desert. We then had to get on camels and travel for twenty more minutes to a large sand dune that lead to a whole underground factory.

This building was something out of a movie. Everything was so high-tech. Ancient Chinese art hung throughout the warehouse. It was like a museum in there. I was the last to arrive. Everybody else had already been seated in the lobby and were waiting to be called. After thirty minutes Wang's son, Lee, escorted us into the conference room without a word.

We were all seated at a large cherry wood table looking at maps of our respective cities. Everybody flew in to meet with the connect. Chris and his homie Jon were from Queens. Some cute brown-skinned Latina's named Sabrina and her cousin Maria were from Miami. Maria was just as cute but a little rough around the edges. X was a middle-aged white man from Los Angeles that came alone like myself.

He didn't talk much so I didn't learn anything about him but I noticed he was similar to me in how he observed the room. X was soaking everything up and taking mental notes. I nodded his way and he nodded back. I could get with that. They all knew of Ramirez and Wang one way or another and were all excited to see what was being offered. I was still a little hesitant about the deal but it was too late. I was in too deep.

"We will be fronting you the $1 million worth of product. That's 50,000 pills in total to start. Once you make that back, you can then make the final decision to stay or go. Is everyone in?" Wang smiled.

"Yes, I'm tryna get paid," the spicy mami, Sabrina, said smiling at me.

"What about protection? What if the pigs try to get us, are we insured in any way?" Chris asked.

"Good question. Yes, but only to an extent. My very good friends at a pharmaceutical company in Guadalajara are making sure that every pill is listed as an acetaminophen since it *does* relieve pain, haha…as to not raise suspicion. You, however, are in charge of your own security measures. In order for this to work we will be unseen but always in contact," Ramirez said never breaking his smile.

I could see everyone in the room tense up with the thought of the feds coming down on us. I remained cool. Along with X. Wang noticed it as he looked us both directly in the eyes.

"When we start getting all this money where we keeping it? I mean a kid from the projects don't just make million-dollar deposits," Jon said lightening the mood some.

"Yeah if it's gonna be move weight and keep laying low like it's always been…then I don't know. Is this gonna help us go legit?" Maria chimed in.

"That's where you have to trust your judgement. We cannot possibly hold your hands. We only meet once a year. To make things easy and less noticeable, each city has a specified date for when you will pay your…joiners fee. Your first—or only—time meeting will be after you sell out this batch," Wang replied.

"65% of the profit will stay with you to be divided among your men and 35% gets paid out to me and Ramirez if you choose to leave after the initial batch. If you stay you keep all 100% of the profit for this batch as a joiner's incentive. If you choose to leave at any time after that you pay the $1 million back plus 15% of any additional earned profit at our yearly meeting and you are done. For good. I'm usually more strategic with my pricing but I think this should be handled differently. We like to pay our men good. Simple enough?" Wang asked.

"Damn 35% is pretty high," Chris said shaking his head.

"Your government takes that out of your taxes and by the time you pay your debts you have even less than the 35% fee. If this is too much for you I have other cities in mind." Wang stated. Lee whispered something in his ear making him chuckle. Wang said something back to him in Mandarin that only he, Ramirez and Lee understood and then faced the group again.

"If you talking shit you can say that in English, b" Chris said growing agitated.

"See father, the blacks are too temperamental," Lee replied cooly looking at all the black men in the room, stopping at me.

"Enough Lee! Now, we will be in touch with you all after you get settled and set up with your new product. If anyone does not wish to continue please speak now," Wang said unbothered by the blatant racism.

Everyone must have heard the same stories that I heard about Ramirez growing up and how he was known to kill anyone who turned their back on him. I assumed Wang was cut from the same cloth. I wasn't surprised no one decided to leave.

We all started chiming in that we were down. Even X started loosening up once he realized there were millions of dollars about to pour in from this deal. Wang explained that this drug was very powerful. Apparently, you could crush it, add it to water and drink it or you could pop it like a perc. I was eager to see how my customers would respond to a new product. I was beginning to see nothing but dollar signs.

"Okay if there aren't any other questions Ramirez, Lee and myself will be in touch with you all about your designated shipment dates. Enjoy the rest of your stay," Wang said as the que for us to leave.

As we walked out I noticed my escort Bo lingered back to talk with Wang for a little. We were all leaving the building and were met by a cool evening breeze. Sabrina caught up to me and nudged my shoulder a little.

"You in Beijing too?" She asked in that sweet accent.

"Yeah," I replied.

"Well then I'm sure you got the VIP passes to that club from Wang. It's our last night…Might as well have some fun. It's supposed to be lit. You going?" she asked.

"Hell," I said in deep thought, "why not?"

***

I decided to keep it simple this night. I wore some fresh Timbs, light distressed jeans, Pop's gold chain that my mom let me have and a Phillies jersey and I already got a fresh cut before I flew out so the waves was on point, ya hear me? I took one last look in the mirror as I brushed my beard. It was around 11pm when Bo hit my jack. Instead of him driving with a partner, he came alone and told me to ride shotgun. We made our way to the club which was right in the center of the city. I was in awe as we drove to our destination. Man, I thought New York in the nighttime was dope. These Chinese cats really knew how to create some shit.

That's what I wanted to do. I wanted to build black communities just like what I was seeing here. I debated about this game I was playing. Unc had me out here all alone to make decisions in a moment's notice. Speaking for my whole team. Peak was going to be what separated us from the regular dope boys. 80s king pin style but even more discreet.

Once Brandon found out I was in Beijing and what I was there for, I knew he would feel a way. He wanted it more than I did and yet here I was. I started to feel myself with that thought. I was the man now. I was getting back to the old me for sure. The me that was ready to move this weight and touch millions with the gang.

As I got out of the truck, Bo said he was partying too. In very broken English he let me know that it would be better to travel with a friend as he tossed the keys to the summo-sized bouncer. Bo was Wang's boy and he was the only native guy besides Lee that I met around my age so far. He dressed like a skater boy which was different than his suit from earlier that day. He seemed more relaxed and had a cool vibe so I nodded as we walked in. I followed him up this dark stairwell that led to a penthouse. People looked at me strange and, no matter how light or yellow I was to the folks back home, I knew the stares were because here I was a black man in the middle of one of the hottest dance clubs in China. I felt like the man though so, I stood by trying to play it cool. A few local chicks walked up to us and started asking Bo questions. He talked back to them and then the girls started smiling at me.

"What did you say to them?" I asked once they left.

Bo smiled, gave me dap and said: "Welcome to the mafia liúmáng."

I figured he didn't say that to the girls but I noticed the stares turned into admiration. I made it my thing to read body language. The men had their guards up but the women were feeling me and that's all that mattered.

The closer we got to our section I understood that Bo was the man around here. It was cool being one of the bros for the night. He spoke the language and had my back. I looked to the bar and saw Sabrina and Maria standing there looking fly laughing with the bartender. Sabrina was dolled up in a dress, make up, curly hair—the whole 9. Maria kept it cool with a sloppy bun and some retro street gear that had her fitting right in with the locals.

"Look I'm about to bag this bitch." I pointed to the bar and Bo nodded his head. He headed to the DJ booth and I made my way through the crowd.

"Wassup Mr. Philly," Sabrina said smiling seductively.

"Oh it's Mr. Philly huh? Don't gas me," I laughed.

"Sabrina, let him breath," Maria laughed, sliding me a shot of tequila.

"Cállate, Maria! Anyway, I got us a section. Come on," Sabrina said grabbing my hand. I looked at Maria and she just laughed and shook her head following behind us. Mami was right at me.

As we all got comfortable in our section and got some drinks flowing, Bo came up to us to see if everything was cool. I let him know I needed some good music to vibe too. He walked back to the DJ and finally some different music started playing. He was mixing in some hip-hop with some disco type stuff so I figured that was better than the other techno music they were playing. Maria found some dudes at the pool table and started making bets in yin, leaving me and Sabrina alone. I liked how these Miami girls rolled.

"So, what you think of this deal?" Sabrina whispered in my ear.

"Seems good to me," I shrugged off. I held her around the waist with one hand and my drink in the other. I was thinking about her body and I wasn't about to talk business right now—especially with a chick I just met.

"Hmm…but don't you think it should be worth more for the risk we're taking?" It was more of a statement than a question so I ignored it.

I started squeezing her hip making her gasp a little. She smiled at me and scooted closer letting the conversation go. We were vibing on a different level and it might have been because of the drinks but I was ready to bust her down.

Sabrina was petit in build. Maybe 5'4" at the most. She was a pretty shade of brown just like her cousin. She had a slim body and her red dress was hugging her hips just right. I was ready for whatever and let it be known.

"Look my man Bo got me. You tryna dip off somewhere?" I asked really feeling my drinks now.

"It's whatever," she smiled drunkenly.

I spotted Bo with some chick and gave him the nod. He walked up to me and whispered over the music:

"Follow me."

I grabbed Sabrina's hand and the drunk girl Bo was dancing with grabbed his arm for balance. We all walked past the pool table and Sabrina let her cousin know we would be back. Bo led us past the bathrooms and into a dim hallway that led to an all-black and gold private room.

Bo opened a safe behind a picture hanging on the wall and started rolling some weed for us to smoke. He tossed his chick a small sandwich bag on a table in front of where she sat on a leather couch. She emptied everything on the table and started snorting a line. I was shocked at how she got right to it in front of complete strangers.

"You made a friend already huh," Sabrina whispered to me.

"Yeah, he's cool, right?" I said motioning Sabrina to come closer to me. Bo's girl asked Sabrina if she wanted some of the powder and Sabrina kindly declined.

After we sat down and the L got passed around a few times between Sabrina, Bo and myself I started rubbing on Sabrina letting her know what time it was and led her to the other couch. In the corner of the room by a mini bar. Sabrina leaned in my lap and got right to business unbuckling my pants and giving me some crazy sloppy. After she was satisfied with how big I got, she stood up and started riding me. She was moaning and screaming out '*Papi!*' I gripped her hips and lifted her up in the air as I stood up. I pounded that pussy when she whispered in between each stroke "come...in...my...mouth...Mr. Philly!"

I put her down, letting her get on her knees to finish what she started. I was so into Sabrina I ain't even peep Bo hitting old girl from the back. She was moaning and making some funny noises that made me and Sabrina crack up. Once we were all satisfied we headed back to our section where Maria had some girl giving her a lap dance.

"Yasss mi hermana!" Sabrina shouted to her cousin.

And so, the party continued.

No matter where I went I had a good time. Beijing was something for the books.

SIX

I caught an early bird flight out of China and got drilled by Unc the second I touched down. I told him everything the connect discussed. How strong the drug was, how we were in to make some good money, my one-night stand with Sabrina and the $1 million worth of pills we were being fronted. Unc wanted to know why I didn't talk Wang down to make things go more in our favor. He wanted more product for a lower amount and said he would get the logistics together later. Unc was the man but I think we both knew there was no talking Wang and Ramirez down.

"Did you try the pill?" he asked.

"Nah, I don't even want those kinds of problems," I responded. Unc smiled, rubbed my head and kept driving.

I didn't say anything about it but Bo slipped me a pill to try it out, but I said I was cool. He told me to keep it and said "do what you want with it," so I did. He sold his pills for double the price but made sure Wang and Ramirez didn't know. That way if he was ever robbed he was never short for the annual meeting. Bo figured they wouldn't miss a couple of dollars. I didn't know why he was helping me out but I took what he was giving out. Bo also did music with some underground Chinks in his hood and let me know his cousin Lin would be coming to the states soon as a foreign exchange student. He was supposed to be staying in the city and Bo asked me to look out for him when he got settled. I gave him my word and also gave him the link to Shook's mixtape.

On Saturday I slept in and it felt good. All the flying and barely getting any sleep had me feeling wore me out. I wanted to run my own test on the pill before we started selling it so I gave the pill to my man Eddy who lived out the county. He was a chemist major in college and had crazy access to labs and shit. He ended up going into security detail with his pops so I figured he was better equipped to check it out. You'd never think he did security though. He was a thin kid with blond hair and always looked timid. Like I said before, he did some little security work for me and the guys here and there and was one of the best assets to my team.

"If this gets out? It's ya ass," I said looking him straight in the eyes as he took the pill from me.

"Chill K-Dot. You know I got you my man," He said already looking at the pill under a microscope. Eddy was about his money too but was on the scamming side of things. Credit cards and social media boutiques. Stuff like that. I didn't want him getting any ideas. We agreed to meet in about two weeks to discuss what he found. I was on the way home so I could start setting up for my cookout when my mom called and asked me to meet at her house. I pulled up to her condo out Lafayette Hill around 3pm.

"Hey baby boy! You just all over the place. I never see you anymore," she frowned walking into the kitchen.

"Chill Ma, I'm right here right now," I laughed.

Karen King could throw down and even though I wasn't hungry I wanted some of whatever she was cooking. I had eaten so much Chinese food over the past few days and needed a home cooked meal.

I sat on the big couch in the living room and rolled a ball back and forth with her yorkie.

"So, as we all know your brother is home and I need you to look out for him," she said checking on some food in the oven.

"I know you ain't ask me to come all the way out here too tell me to look out for B," I said shaking my head.

"Not just that…I also happen to miss my baby. I don't see you as much with your career and businesses and women—"

"Okay Ma I get it," I laughed.

"So, what you been up to B-Boy? You getting to the money or what?" she joked. She mentioned before that 'B-Boy' was a corny nickname. The fellas used it and she always called me that when she was hyping me up.

"I'm doing alright. The lounge is almost done, I'm just waiting on one more investor. I'm getting a lot more buzz with Shook too."

"Your artist, right?" she smiled.

"Yeah that's right. We gonna blow up Ma, I can feel it."

"Good…your dad would be so proud of you baby. Olly would have been so proud of how you're turning out. Now if I could get some of that to rub off on Brandon I would be at peace," she said flagging her hand in the air.

I turned the TV on to a little league baseball game and China was playing against Mexico. I was brought back to a few nights ago when me and Bo had the club going up! Then I thought about what Ma was saying and I started to feel guilty that she didn't know what I was really getting into. As far as she was concerned I was an angel.

"Bran is cool. He's a little wild but he's smart," I said trying to calm her down when she brought him up again. Brandon had a way of getting her so worked up. He caught a lot of punches in the chest back in the day because of it.

"Yeah, you're right baby. I have to stop worrying about him. He's a grown ass man. Anyway, how's my girl Maya doing?" she asked referring to Uptown. I honestly couldn't tell her because I had been ignoring her lately. I just wasn't feeling her anymore but knew Mom loved her so I said:

"She's cool."

"*She's cool.*" she mimicked. "What does that even mean? I swear my boys drive me crazy!" She faced the ceiling rolling her eyes all dramatic.

"What Ma? She's cool. What you want me to say?"

"That you're settling down and giving me some grandbabies," she said getting plates out the cabinets.

"Whoa! What's up with you? No kids, no thanks," I laughed.

We talked some more over lunch. She made some baked chicken, yellow rice, cabbage and cornbread. My favorite meal from her. I wanted to know what she wanted but I let her take her time.

"Brett baby, I'm out here alone and you know I can't tell you and your brother what to do…well you know all this. Just promise me if he tries to make you do anything for him you'll tell him no," she said now looking me in the eyes very seriously.

"Ma, where is all this coming from?" I asked as if I was confused.

"I had a dream that Bran was selling for your uncle Allen again and you got hurt really bad because of it," she said getting quiet with tears in her eye. I only seen Ma cry once and that was when Pop died…her pride wouldn't let the tears fall but she was clearly shaken up.

"Ma, I was just with both of them last night, just hanging. We cool. If he was selling anything I think I would know. Plus, you the fairy Godfather. You got all the connections in the city I think you would know something before I did," I said shrugging off the conversation.

"Brett, promise me."

"Promise you what Ma?"

"Brett Solomon King! Promise me you will not be out here selling no damn narcotics with AJ and that you will watch your brothers back. I worked too hard for—"

"Ma, chill I got you, we chillin'," I said looking away from her. I couldn't look her in the eyes and lie.

"Yeah okay Mr. Chilling. That's all you say '*I'm chillin' Ma. Everything chillin' Ma,*'" she said rolling her eyes.

Whatever the dream was must have scared her bad and I tried my best to assure her that everything was cool. Nothing got past Ma! She always said God let her know what her children were up to and how she could sense danger and blessings when they were coming our way. I didn't really understand what she meant but she assured me when I had my own kids I would start to understand a mother's love.

I kicked it with her for a little bit more and took a plate to go. I also reminded her not to forget the party at my crib the next day. I wanted everybody to be there. It was birthday season and this was kicking things off just right. I finally got back to my crib and decided to lay low for the rest of the night. I posted a video to remind everyone that the cookout was still on. All of the fellas were in charge of something and I made sure everybody had their tasks locked in. Simone and—I assumed—the whole city was coming out for my day party and I wanted it to be a good time, you know? This would be the calm before I got back on my hustle for real.

***

Sunday rolled around and by 12:30pm the sun was shining bright, folks started showing up, and the city was feeling alive. Everybody on my block caught wind I was throwing a cookout and decided they wanted to pull their grills and music out too, so we turned it into a block party. Plus Shook asked could him and his crew bring their dirt bikes out to do a video. It was about to be a zoovie.

Man, it was nothing like a Sunday afternoon in the hood. I decided to keep it chill and wore my man's clothing line *No Opposition*, just a simple black tee with gold writing. I wore all that with some black distressed jean shorts, some white Nike tube socks and my yellow and black foams. Oh, and Pop's gold chain of course.

"Looking good baby boy. Just like ya daddy. God rest his soul. He would be so proud!" Ms. Jones smiled as she sipped some fresh iced tea.

Ms. Jones lived next door to me and always looked out with small stuff like taking care of my lawn. She was the grandma of the block. I always gave her some money once a month and she never mentioned what she saw or heard at my place. I warned her about how big the party would be. She flagged me off and let me know just because she was 70 years old didn't mean she didn't know how to party.

"B-Boy what's good?" Jeff from across the street called out as he saw people start pulling up. I managed to get majority of the block to sign the party permit so I didn't even need his mom's signature.

"Wassup," I said not giving him too much play. He was 40 and gossiped more than the ladies.

"Shit about to hit the lid out here. I'm a slide through with a bottle or something later." He was trying to be cool in front of some girls walking down the block.

"Yeah okay," I laughed.

I set D up on the porch so he could man the grill next to Jay and Shook's DJ booth. Brandon and Shawn had a game of Spades going in front of my house with some girls they invited. Dina and Shayla were inside cooking the food, and a few other close people stopped by for a bit and chilled inside the house. And of course, the hoes! They was everywhere daaawg! All kinds of flavors and sizes. We always brought the city out and if she was a baddie living in my city? One of the guys in the gang had her!

D was trying to bag some feisty Rican jawn and asked me to make sure Dina didn't bring anymore meat out for the grill just yet. I told him I could stall for ten minutes but that was it and headed to the kitchen. Dina was in her catering zone and I wasn't trying to get in her way. We all knew she was a crazy Rican herself and if he got caught I did NOT want to be in the hot seat.

"Wassup Brett," Uptown said hugging me from behind.

"Who is this and where my homegirl at?" Shayla said with an eyebrow raised. *Come on Shay…and whyyy is this girl here?*

Ignoring Shayla, because I didn't know how to answer that, I simply said: "Wassup," and gave Uptown a quick hug.

"I'm Maya, his bestfriend…Who are you?" Uptown said turning red. She was sick, ha.

"Oh, that's what y'all call ya'll women these days? Well, that's news. Brett told me he was a playa for life. Niggas always lying," Shayla laughed punching me on my arm. It was meant to look playful but that shit hurt. *Really Shay?*

"Anyway, Brett. Your mom told me y'all was having a cookout and thought I should come with her. Some of my girls met me here—if that's cool with you," she smiled. I could never resist her smile. She was a beautiful girl. I just couldn't allow myself to give in to her anymore.

"Of course, whatever you want," I said looking to see what Dina was working on.

"BRETT!"

"Why are you hovering over me boy? And why are you in here? Back up!" Dina said swatting my hand away when I went to taste the seafood salad.

"BRETT!" *Gotta be Ma.*

"You don't hear somebody calling you? Back up little boy," Dina said, knocking my had away again making me drop a piece of shrimp.

I could tell Uptown was irritated by my nonchalant attitude towards her but she wasn't about to get no play, man. I really didn't want her around. She missed me and I can't lie—I missed her too. But I had to give her the cold shoulder. It was no other way.

45

I walked outside to see my mom chilling on a lawn chair with another neighbor of mines. "Baby Brett," Ma said giving me a kiss on the cheek.

"Hey Ma,"

"You see Maya?" she smirked.

"Yeah Ma," I said returning a fake smile.

I walked around the side of the house where a few chicks gave me a hug. They were asking me to get them a drink, to show off in front of their friends. Of course, I got them a drink as I laughed to myself soaking up all the attention. For the next few hours Uptown kept alternating between coming outside or sending a friend to spy on me, but I didn't care.

Around 4:30 pm the older folks started leaving and everybody else started falling through. At that point, me and the gang were taking pictures and doing small cameo videos. Shook had a few drinks and was finally in movie mode. I respected his grind and let him have full creative control.

While all that was going on, I was starting to think Simone forgot about the cookout.

"Yo Shay!" I yelled inside.

"She out back!" Dina answered.

"What fool? Don't you see grown folks talking?" Shay snapped. Apparently, she was rekindling an old fling. I later found out the bul Fling was her high school sweetheart and that Ms. Jones, my neighbor, was his great aunt. Small world.

"Fuck outta here Shay-Shay. Yo you talk to Mone?" I asked.

"Yeah she just texted me and said she's on her way Mr. Pressed. Now shoo fly," she laughed.

About thirty minutes had passed when I spotted Simone walking down the street with two identical twins that looked just like her. Simone's friend Char was following behind them taking selfies. You would have thought the twins were Char's sisters and not Mone's because of their sandy brown hair color and light skin tone but those faces were Simone all the way.

"Dammmn! Who the hell is them bitches right there in the sundresses?" D said taking his shades off.

"Sheesh I can tell they asses fat from the front, gotdamn," Jay chimed in dapping Shawn up.

I told my camera guy to catch them walking up in slow motion. Shit was coming together perfectly.

"I want Tia and Tamera," Brandon said getting off the spades table while Jay and Shawn followed behind. Brandon and Tina were arguing again which was his way of making her stay home so he could use the car. The girls at the spades table were pissed how all the guys completely ignored them but there was nothing they could do.

46

I just sat back and laughed as Simone and her crew rolled their eyes—flagging everybody off. Some girls were whispering to each other with frowned up faces as Simone walked right up to me.

"Boss Baby got it litty on a Sunday, huh?" she cheesed.

"Wassup Mone, thanks for coming," I said giving her a hug.

Not letting her waist go, I was introduced to her two little sisters, Anita and Aisha, and her homegirl Char. I knew of Char. She was the round-the-way girl that everybody loved, but it was nice to be formally introduced.

Mone and Char made a dope pair. I let them know where everything was and to help themselves. Char made eye contact with Shook but tried to keep it cool. She recognized a few faces so, she made sure Mone was cool and then made her way through the crowd with the twins following behind her.

"So, wassup mama?" I said as me and Mone walked to the side of my house.

"Nothing much. I gotta be honest, I kinda missed you at work," she said throwing a playful punch at me.

"Why you always wanna play," I laughed dodging a hit.

"Because I can," she giggled throwing another punch I let fall.

"You goofy as shit what you laughing at?" I was amused.

"Nothing...I guess I'm glad I came," she blushed.

"What you getting into after this?"

"I don't know. I got my aunt car for tonight so I'm gonna drop the girls off when they ready and then I don't know after that," she said looking in her bag. She looked around and asked was it cool to light her blunt. I told her she could do whatever she wanted.

"What you mean?" she laughed.

"What's mines is yours,"

"Oh, whatever Brett," she giggled.

I put my cup down on the window ledge and grabbed her around the waist. She relaxed her body into mines and started rubbing her gold locket necklace. I opened up the locket and saw a picture of a light-skin, older version of Simone. The same light face the twins had.

"That's the big homie...that's Mama. She was beautiful right?" she said as I closed it. Not protesting all the attention that I was giving her, Mone laid her head on my chest.

"Yes, she was," I responded taking a sip from my red cup. I offered her some and she drank a little.

Mone was looking good with her long ponytail and gold rimmed glasses. She wore a white strapless sundress and some gold platform sandals that gave her a few extra inches. She was looking simple but sexy.

"This white against ya skin is nice," I whispered in her ear.

"Oh yeah?" she whispered back.

"Look at the lovebirds," Shayla laughed walking up behind us.

47

"How long were you standing there, old lady?" Mone laughed.

"No this heifer did not!" Shayla giggled moving me out the way so they could hug.

"Dang Shay. Didn't you tell me 'shoo fly' earlier?" I asked giving her a little nudge on the shoulder.

"Oh, hush up Brett and how many times I gotta tell you that I fight dudes? Pushing on me. Monie this white is doing something for that chocolate skin baby girl," Shayla exclaimed snapping her fingers.

Somebody started calling my name and when I showed my irritation they both started laughing.

"Go host ya party, King. Shay-Shay walk with me I need to check on my sisters. They just turned 21 and they wildin' out," she said as they disappeared in the backyard...

WHOOP! WHOOP!

Once the sun disappeared behind the foggy night sky, red and blue lights flashed at the end of my block signaling it was time to shut things down. Everybody was booing and taking pictures of themselves in front of the cop cars. We made sure to get that on camera too before we wrapped things up.

The cops cleared everyone out but a few folks still stuck around. Dina was letting D be great and went home which was cool. Mone wasn't ready to go so me and D matched with her and one of the girls from the spades table and we had a crazy cypher. The twins and Char were dancing to some music that Shook was playing for them. We finished smoking and Simone sat on the railing with Shay as they laughed and joked with Ms. Jones and Shay's old boo.

I sat on my steps next to where Simone was and leaned my head on her thigh.

"Get yo sweaty ass head off that pretty little girl's dress. Like she don't got white on," Ms. Jones laughed. She caught some contact from our cypher and was biddin' right with us.

"Chill Mama J, this my baby right here," I replied.

"Mmhmm. I can tell. Y'all been boo'd up all night," Ms. Jones smiled with a wink.

"You good, King?" Mone asked rubbing my hair.

"Yeah I'm chillin'. You ready for work tomorrow?"

"Work? Oh, hell no Brett it's only 8:30 I don't want to think about work just yet," Shayla interjected making Simone laugh. The two winked at each other and bust out laughing leaving the rest of us confused. I was so drunk I laughed too.

"Who got you kee-keeing out here?" Ma said as she walked out the house with Uptown following behind her.

"Brett and Bran, I'm leaving. I love y'all—be safe. Brett don't let all these people stay in ya house tonight either. Good night everybody," Ma said waving.

"I got you Ma," I said giving her a hug.

By this point she had a few drinks and started dancing with Mone's little sisters. Uptown's irritation was showing as she looked Simone and her crew up and down a few times. Uptown said goodnight to the guys, did a little too much with Jay to try and get to me and walked past me without saying a word. *Perfect.*

"Why you bring her?" I asked after Uptown was in the car.

"Because I didn't want to ride by myself and Maya was sweet enough to take this ride with me. So, I told her to invite a friend or two," she said with a grin.

"Goodnight Ma," I said walking away.

"Love you too baby boy," she laughed. She said goodnight again to everyone and got in her car. Once they pulled off everybody got back to what they were doing…

"Ard Brett I'm getting out of here," Simone said as her sisters started walking back to their car.

"Okay baby girl. I'm a walk you."

It was around 11pm at this point and the block was pretty quiet except for a few houses that were still partying. It was me, the gang, Mone and her crew left.

"I had fun, you had the whole city out here any nobody got hurt," she said reaching in her bag for her keys.

"Oh, for sure…you still don't know what you doing after this?" I asked.

"Yeah, I'm gonna head home…work in the morning and shit," she said about to get in the car. I could see the twins staring from the backseat trying to hear what was going on. Shorty mood was different and I figured she peeped how close Uptown and Ma was.

"Okay, that's cool…can I have a hug? Give me some love you bouta just pull off and shit," I said pulling her into my arms. She tried to pull away but I wasn't having it.

"What happened just that quick?" I asked squeezing her all over making sure to feel on her ass. *Damn she soft.*

"Nothing, King…" Mone said warming up to my hug. She was trying not to smile but come on, it was me.

"Oh ard. Text me when you get home," I kissed her on the cheek and waited until her and her girls pulled off.

"You still get all the bad bitches, huh?" Jeff said to me as he crossed the street.

"I just be chilling."

"Yeah you still the man after all these years," he replied walking up the steps to his house. I didn't respond after that but I wondered how long he was watching me at Simone's car. I let it go and sat on the porch blowing down another blunt with the guys.

SEVEN

Two weeks later…

It was the night before we finally got the call from Wang and Ramirez when I got with Eddy to see what was up with this new drug. I pulled up to the mini mansion around 9pm. He stayed with his mom and dad after college and because they didn't kick him out he didn't see any reason to leave. He had the whole basement to himself and they made it sound proof for him. Pretty good living if you ask me.

"Bro this shit is wild," he said eyes wide as he let me in.

"I know," I smiled. But he wasn't smiling back.

"What's wrong?" I asked feeling tense.

"Dog, this shit is stronger than crack but subtler. Where the fuck did you get this from? You know what? Don't even answer that," he said closing the door behind me.

"A guy I know sells all kinds of stuff to the high-school kids," Eddy said sitting down at his computer. Next to him was a lab table where he had the pill broken down into small pieces under one microscope and some white powder under another.

"Damn he selling dog food to the kids?" I asked.

"He's in high school himself. I think his dad is into it. But yeah, so, I got some coke. I needed it for comparisons. I had to use a lot more coke to match the potency of this pill though," he continued typing all kinds of codes to log into one system.

"E-Dog, get to the point man." I said irritated. Eddy wasn't one for small talk.

"Look at this." He pointed to a video on his computer, ignoring my impatience. "I got four mice and made two small houses. One for the pill exhibits and the other for the coke. I kept them fed of course but started feeding them the drugs little by little for the past few days. The ones on the cocaine started scratching at the windows and pushing food away when I took it away for a day. But the ones on the pill were fine. Like they could function for a little bit without it," he

50

said showing clips of videos he took. He was getting more excited the more he talked. He was on a roll so I didn't interject. "What got weird is, after 2 days went by, they got very violent with each other if they didn't have the fix they needed from the pill. They were trying to kill each other bro. That was Monday…" He grew silent as we watched the video. The mice were really fighting each other because they wanted more product. I had mixed feelings. I didn't want to feed my people this poison but the rush of getting money I hadn't touched yet already overwhelmed me.

"How the fuck did somebody make this? I tried to make a replica pill as best I could in the small amount of time I had and fed it to the mice. It was like giving dirt to a loud smoker. They were cool for a few hours but they were back at each other's heads again. See, they're still fighting each other and they look a little skinny. They won't eat unless the pill is mixed in.

"I was able to lookup some of the ingredients and where they came from. Some of the ingredients in this shit are banned in almost every country," he continued.

"Something else is mixed in but it's majority plant extracts. I figured out the coordinates of where this plant could possibly grow. It's coming up as somewhere in a desert. Somewhere in China. But I hit a wall because the websites are blocked for that country. The only desert I could think of was the Tennger Desert. But another plant is coming out of Mexico somewhere. And that's as far as I got when you called me and said you were on the way. I don't know how your secret friend made this shit but they are dealing with some high-level shit, bro." I could tell he was exhausted from all of his hard work.

"Did you take some of that pill?" I questioned.

"No way! I only do weed, bro. I'm not putting that crap in my body. I know some people who would love to cop up around here. These kids do stuff city kids are too scared to even touch," he stated.

"Okay, good." I responded taking in everything I just learned.

"Plans on getting rich huh?" he asked.

I slid him his hard-earned money. Five stacks in total. He always gave me a discount so I figured this time I would pay full price. He looked at me and gave a slight smirk then nodded his head. He put his money in a safe under his desk. As always, I turned and let him handle his business in private.

I had a long time to think on that flight back in. Eddy was the only one who could make sure I had a legit security detail. If I was going to be the regular 9-5 guy—who ran a lounge—I needed Eddy in on this. I figured this was the perfect time to tell him my plan.

"Look E-Dog, we go back to chasing chicks on campus and selling weed to the underclassmen. Maybe you could join my team. I need the good shit. I know you can get it. I'm talking guards, guns, ammo, security cameras for me and the guys cribs and businesses. Oh, and new stash houses. Then you reach out to your mans out here and see if he wants to buy some work from us. I'll pay you for throwing the oop," I said sliding him another stack.

He leaned back in his chair and thought long and hard just staring at the money on the desk.

"Ard man. I'm in. I'll let you know by tonight about my friend," he said shaking my hand.

"You in now, White Boy. Get caught and you the lone man standing. Snitch and…well, you know. Let's get this money E," I said dapping him up before leaving out.

I pulled up to my crib and sat in the car remembering all the cities that were invited to China. All poor neighborhoods. New day, new drug—same concept. It was killed or be killed. At this point I got myself so mentally prepared to sell this shit that I didn't know what to do. Maybe I shouldn't have looked into it. Maybe Eddy would rat on me one day. These were all the risk I was willing to take for the love of the money.

***

The next day we got the call that the shipment would be in that night. Brandon, D, Shawn and myself got together and headed to the warehouse in one of D's white construction vans. We pulled into a lot right off of 95 South by the airport around 10pm. Brandon wasn't happy D was in on the plan but if this was to work I needed all hands-on deck. A strong army.

When we pulled up to the gate, the armed guard didn't say much. He pointed to the end of the strip where the pick-up spot was and let D, who was driving, know we had no more than 8 minutes for the transaction. D just nodded. The gate opened and we turned right and went to the end of the strip as instructed. We hopped out, said hey to the truck drivers, grabbed the four boxes and put them in the back of the van. From there we drove to one of the stash houses Eddy set up for us near Tina's crib out Frankford. Once inside the basement, we had Unc's two young girls help us divide the shipment into red plastic prescription bottles and vacuum seal packs like breath mints. Unc had one of the young girls pour all of us a shot but before we took it, of course he was grilling me on how everything went down and dapped me up as his way of saying good job. I noticed Brandon rolled his eyes and started telling Unc how he's ready to move this weight.

"Good shit, B. I'm glad to know you all in," Unc said rubbing Brandon's head.

"Ard, youngin's, listen up. Y'all remember how we used to do it back in the day. I'm laying low this time around. I can't be all hands on and shit. D and Shawn y'all been around long enough to know how we roll. Get caught and you the lone man standing. Snitch and…well, you know. Let's get this money young bloods." He lifted up his shot glass as a toast.

We all took the shot, played some music and continued dividing up the product. By the looks on everyone's faces, we all knew this was some heavy shit but we were all looking to get paid. Scared money don't make no money, you know?

KAREN'S INTERLUDE

Spring of 2007…

Brett was finishing out his sophomore year of high school at Lafayette Hill Prep and was the head of the business club. He applied everything he'd learned in the streets to growing his club and was running a financially successful organization. It was getting so much attention that even the mayor came to see what the hype was all about. Karen knew that her baby boy was destined for greatness.

Brandon on the other hand started acting out in school and was always stealing the car to drive to the city. He just wanted to hang around his no-good cousins. They weren't blood related but King's nonetheless and were always getting into trouble with the law. Karen's presence was still felt in the city so Brandon avoided jail for a long time. Being the widow of Oliver King gave her more pull than anyone could have imagined. Her late husband was one of the biggest underground kingpins the city had ever seen and people were still surviving off of the fruits of his labor.

The city mourned when Oliver died. The same streets he ran were the same ones to take him out. At least that's how she dealt with it. All her friends tried to convince her to come back home where she knew people but Karen didn't want to see any of their faces. She knew the killer was still out there. The sad part was as many families as Oliver fed, no one would help her find the killer. Old detective friends would come through for her with anything else but would not touch his murder case. She chalked it as the city not wanting to help because solving his murder would unravel some corrupt cops and city workers. Plus, all the no snitching rules that she was well aware of still applied. No one saw Olly the way she saw him. To her he was the love of her life. A family man. But to everyone else? Just another dead hustler.

In Karen's world, Oliver was the man in the streets, but she soon learned the streets were hell and once one top guy fell from the throne another younger guy was ready to take their place. With

Brandon acting out, Brett always being so shy and timid—the depressed widow was at her wits end!

"How the hell am I gonna raise two strong men without you, baby? Two black men at that..." She would cry to herself.

Karen was so used to her comfortable living that she didn't know what to do with herself. She would have a nice drink from time to time and chose to lay low with the three million dollar stash Olly left her. She didn't want to raise any suspicions by still living in their mansion so after thinking long and hard over wine and tears, she downsized to a nice condo in a quiet neighborhood with people who minded their business and didn't know her.

None of the remaining Kings were used to this life they now had to live either. Karen was from the hood but it was nothing like getting on and then getting knocked back down to reality. Her new neighborhood wasn't bad but it wasn't her home she planned to grow old in with the love of her life. She was so concerned about how her sons would grow without their dad. As a last-ditch effort, she made Brandon attend bible study with her and put Brett in boxing classes to help him be more confidant. He was more of a "I want some milk and cookies" than a "catch a girl freak a girl" kind of boy like his big brother. Brandon refused to go back after two meetings and Brett always cried about getting hit too hard during his weekly spar sessions.

The strong survived and punks didn't last. Karen loved her babies and wanted them to grow and be strong men who didn't end up murdered like their father. She finally put her feelings aside and reached out to AJ who had seemed to calm down in more recent years after his baby brother died. He appeared to be a changed man so she let him know she needed his help. He was Karen's last hope.

She'd met AJ first at a night club back in the day. They had a little fling but that didn't last more than two weeks. She didn't want anybody to know she was dealing with him but she had to admit he always paid the bills and sexed her like crazy. At the time Karen was still a hairdresser at her home girl Trish's shop called Kutz. They specialized in short hair and the ladies and the fella's were constantly booking Trish and Karen so they could get fly before party's every Friday night. The ladies offered everything from traditional cuts and low curls to the trendier A-symmetrical and finger wave styles over the years so money was always to be made. Whatever you needed they did it. Local celebrities even stopped by the shop to see these two young girls that could cut better than some of the guys.

AJ was always managing a few hustles at the time and brought his little brother, Oliver, by the shop one day as his wing-man so he could discuss business with Trish. AJ saw the shop as a cash cow and wanted a piece while it was still gaining some recognition in the city to help clean his drug money.

56

he got locked up for his 1st misdemeanor offense and was scheduled to be released in a few months. In the meantime, AJ needed a new muscle man to get his dirty work done. Some young punk was trying to take over one of AJ's blocks and had already robbed his stash house where Brett and his friend Shawn were chilling with some young girls. AJ couldn't have that. He was mad Brett didn't kill the thief where he stood but knew his nephew just wasn't built like that. This was AJ's opportunity to make a man out of Brett.

AJ caught the young thief zoned out from drinking too much lean one night. AJ walked up on him and before the young guy could grab his piece, AJ knocked him out with the butt of his pistol and dragged him into an alley where he was parked. He lifted the young man up into the trunk of his pick-up truck and drove him off to the warehouse where they dealt with people who were disloyal or went against the King family.

The young guy's name was Maj. He was a high school dropout that just had a baby and started slinging to feed his new family. He was also sending money to his girl that was still in college. She planned to graduate from a popular HBCU in a year and he was going to move with her and their daughter.

By the time AJ's crew got done beating the boy up, nobody could make out what he was saying. His mouth had scotch tape with dried blood all over it. He was crying and begging Brett, who held Maj at gunpoint, not to pull the trigger. What right did Brett have to take Maj's life? In the streets, Uncle AJ always said, there was no room for those kinds of emotions. It was all about the money, power and respect. Brett never caught a body and AJ knew that this would toughen him up.

"Nigga time is money! This nigga a McCoy and he mad we eating. Real mad. He so mad that he held you at gun point to take ya food! He tried to take us out youngin. Kill this motherfucker!" Uncle AJ yelled out.

BLAT! BLAT! BLAT!

Maj's brains were splattered all over the ground behind him with his eyes wide open. Brett's right hand was shaking and he felt the wind get knocked out of him. He just took another man's life for the first time. None of Uncle AJ's lessons in the woods along the Schuylkill River trail could prepare Brett for the smell of a man defecating on himself for the last time or the smell of burnt flesh where the bullets entered the body. Maj tried to kill Brett at the stash house that night and all Brett thought about was who Maj left behind. Another baby would grow up without their father because of the game…

AJ instructed Brett to clean up and dump the body in the river after nightfall. He also instructed Brett on how to tie the cement blocks to Maj's ankles and along his body. Brett wanted to throw up but didn't want to be a punk so he finished the job to make his uncle proud.

Later that night Karen could see the empty look in her baby boys face as he finished his homework and went to bed without eating. She was too fearful to ask what was wrong as she remembered the look Olly had when he took out a good friend of his for being disloyal. Karen didn't want to think he was involved in anything illegal so she let it go but never forgot the fear that gripped her heart because of it.

EIGHT

August 12, 2015…Birthday Bash…

Yo it's ya boy Shook! Y'all we got some fine ladies in the place AND it's the big homies birthday. So, because of that I wanted to make tonight very special. B-Boy finally gave the green light on the twerk contest for a two-thousand-dollar cash prize. I think cause it's birthday season…" he said getting drowned out by the young hype crowd.

As I gave dap to my bouncer, Brick, I looked to the stage and smiled as I watched my youngin really work the crowd. All the girls were smiling and pointing out which friend should go up for the reward money. It wasn't my style but Shook had this hosting thing down to a science. Every other Friday night at the lounge so far was pulling in a lot of bread so I finally let up and let him do his contest.

My youngin' was up next! He had some ways to go but he was young and ready to take on the world. Shook was really taking his music serious and was using the lounge as a marketing tool to get his face out there. I was connected with some guys in the underground music scene and got them to put Shook in some of their cyphers. He was getting buzz for killing anybody that stepped to him on the mic and Friday nights were turning out exactly how I planned.

The D&K Lounge was located in Cheltenham off of 19th Street by the smoke shop we always got our hookah from. Me and D rode past the abandoned lot for a while and one day decided to go half on it. D was the construction guy so he got his crew together and from there the empire started. It was just a small spot at first but once we started getting this money and paying promoters and shit, we got the okay to buy the next building, tore the wall down and made one big lounge. Some haters, like Brandon, thought the location wouldn't work but I always defied the odds.

Every 1st and 3rd Friday was talent night and of course Shook was in charge of the entertainment. One stack per night. He was a good kid and I knew he could use the two thousand a month to help his family. It was my business proposal in exchange for him to truly stay out the streets and focus on the music. He figured he made okay change with me and got to do what he loved. Which brought me more money. A win-win.

Honestly though, with this new product money wasn't even a problem. Just a few months—weeks really—had passed since we introduced Peak to the hood and we were already eating very well because of it. With Eddy being our lookout, things were rolling good with no interruptions. Wang and Ramirez promised the customers would love it and they promised it would be some money we never seen. They were right. We were the only ones in the city that had it so you know we had the hood and the suburbs going crazy. I thought I was eating before but now I felt like a king for real. We were stuffing bread in the damn attacks and floor boards! D kept saying the money was oming in too fast but I wasn't complaining. Too much money was a good problem to me. I really couldn't complain about anything. Well there was just one thing...

I had to slow down a bit with Mone. She was still off and on with her dude so the good guy in me had to let her do her thing. I let her know where I stood and whenever she was ready I would be there. I'm a sucka right? Yeah, I know. I was playing chess not checkers as my pops would say...

"Yo! It's $20 fam," Stace said to Always Short.

Always Short was a oldhead who always tried to finesse one of our bartenders. He would open up a tab every Friday night but was always short and would never tip. I let him keep coming back but D hated bul.

"You better be glad Brett even giving ya white ass a chance in here," Short's girl said rolling her eyes.

"You know what? Yo! D! Handle this please?" Stace said as she walked away to get the bottle girls ready for VIP.

"Short, it's just $20 you got that, right?" D said looking irritated.

"Delando don't try to play me. Respect ya elders. You know I'm getting to the money. I told White Girl open up a tab and—"

"Not tonight nigga. Pay the fuck up or get the fuck out," D told him.

"Ayo Brett! Birthday boy! Help a nigga out. You know we go way back!" Short yelled over the music. I just laughed and headed to my office. *Not tonight...*

***

Unc was in VIP talking to one of his young girls like always and then dipped off for the night once he got a call from one of his homies. Lounges weren't his twist but he knew it meant a lot to me for him to show up.

63

"Yo! Lil bro this place really the shit. I guess y'all really doing y'all thing," Brandon said looking around my office as I locked my gun in the safe. My office aka The Pad was right in front of the dance floor but no one on the outside knew it was tinted and that I could see everything. It came equipped with a futon, mini bar and a pool table.

"Thanks bro I appreciate it. Heads up—don't touch the girls," I jokingly warned. I was about to show him to the Rasta themed room with the private dancers. I ain't need no haters telling nobody I was running a whore house or something. You'd be surprised how many folks tried to get my place shut down on some nut type time and we just opened up shop.

Brandon discussed moving the weight in a little more detail and how he felt D had too much say. I switched it up and talked about the Sixers and the draft class. I ain't feel like discussing all that other shit here. Especially on my birthday. This was the one place I could go and just have a good time.

Everybody was eating too good too fast to have any beef right now. Brandon was spending money like it would never run out. Losing it to dumb bets and drinking lean but wanted to be worried about the next man. You couldn't tell him anything, though. Even Unc couldn't get through to him. I was just trying to keep my promise to Ma and kept an eye on him.

I eventually made my way back out front, stood at the DJ booth and thanked everybody for coming out. I let everybody know it was open bar for 2 hours making Stace roll her eyes and smile. Her tips were always good during open bar but the people started rushing her like crazy with request. It was a good fucking night!

"Happy birthday LL!" I heard a voice shout from behind me.

"Hey! What are you doing here?" I was surprised to see Simone as I turned around. *This night can't get any better.*

"My girl Char fuck with your boy Shook now so she asked me and the twins to come through. I promise I'm not stalking you," she laughed.

"Wouldn't be the first time…I can't say it would bother me though," I winked.

After talking about work for a little, I told her that everything was on me that night and reminded her about open bar. I let her know she could order whatever she wanted. Food, hookah—whatever her girls wanted. I got a worker to set up another section that hadn't been sold and got some wristbands letting Mone know VIP was open to her and her crew. She smiled, said thanks and let her girls know what was up.

Some other ladies who were loyal to Uptown remembered Simone from the cookout and started rolling their eyes and stuff. Mone and her crew made their VIP grand entrance and didn't pay the haters any mind. I decided to join them with Shook and we got the shots and pictures rolling. Like anything in life, you know you can't have that good of a time without something fucking up.

"Sooo, you give ya new little girlfriend wristbands for VIP but you flee me for the past few months. Sooo, what? This ya new shorty or something?" Uptown said standing on the side of the VIP rope. *Not tonight…*

"You need me to leave y'all two alone?" Mone said getting in her professional mode like we were at work or something. I was so buzzed by this point any filter I had left was gone.

"Fuck no, babe. No, this ain't my shorty, Maya. You ain't neither. Go 'head. You making yourself look bad," I said trying to be nice. Like, how you standing outside the VIP area getting loud? She knew I ain't roll like that so I needed her to walk away before she got embarrassed.

"Ohhh…so that's how we doing things? Cool. Like say less, nigga, say less. You really weird as shit. She's pretty for a dark-skin girl, I guess. I hope you know he ain't shit," she said staring angrily at Simone. *She really putting on a show.*

Mone just laughed and said: "I think you better listen to your boy and go head before you get embarrassed by this dark-skin girl."

Uptown looked at Simone and then me. I don't know what she was thinking about but she looked like she was ready to pounce on Simone. If I didn't want her before, I really didn't want her now. She already knew I was around and had my women. I wasn't looking for anything. That was my disclaimer. Do with it what you want.

She turned to me and said, "you really like this one," shook her head and walked away. *Man…whatever…*

Mone didn't even mention it. She carried on as if this was something she was used to. Char saw the tension and started giving Shook drunk ass a lap dance while holding onto Mone's arm. Just like that we got back to partying.

I didn't realize how much time had passed. It couldn't have been more than 7 song changes when I heard:

POP! POP! POP! Followed by:

"HE'S GOT A GUN!"

For five long minutes it was complete chaos. The DJ didn't even think to stop the music before he dipped so it was loud and crazy. The place was filled past capacity because it was my birthday so I knew everybody wouldn't be able to get out in a good amount of time. Both my security guards that were in VIP ran towards the commotion on the dance floor and started helping people get out safely. I grabbed Mone's hand and Shook grabbed Char. Mone's sisters and a few other females from another section followed behind us. We all left out the back where the staff parked. I was looking for Brandon and D but they weren't around. I gave Mone my keys and told her to wait in my car. I could tell she was scared but calmly told her sisters she was going to ride with me. They were hesitant but she promised she would call them when she was in.

"Yo, King you need my boys to handle this?" Shook asked as Char and the twins hopped in his old SUV. He was always ready to go to war for me and I respected that. But I needed him to worry about the music.

"Naw we good man, get these girls home," I stated.

"But Brett I can handle this quick—no questions," he said with loyalty in his eyes.

I shook my head and gave Simone one more glance. Shook chewed his cheek and lowered his head in frustration, then told me be safe. I went back inside the main area of the lounge in a matter of seconds where I saw people still jamming the two emergency exits and the main entrance.

"B-Boy! We gotta get outta here somebody came in with a gun. I couldn't find you! We still got way too many people in here man!" D yelled.

"Where's Brandon?" I asked walking back towards the Rasta room. I stopped midway to see if my staff had stuck to the emergency plan and took the hidden cellar steps under the bar.

I heard some more gunshots and felt D reach for me but before I could react, three bullets ripped through my left arm, shoulder and chest. They had to have come from somewhere near the entrance because it hit me from behind. D was facing the same way I was so I think he was just grabbing me on some big brother shit. I grabbed my chest and hit the ground. The music was so loud, I couldn't hear anything. People were screaming and I was scared I would get trampled. I couldn't tell who the shooter even was. I just knew I was losing blood and I was losing it fast. I couldn't see or hear anybody but my phone was in my hand so, I hit my recent calls button and dialed 1.

"Ma...I'm at the lounge near you. Help..."

***

"We need everybody out of the way!" I heard a lady rudely yell snapping me from a dream of the night I caught my first body.

I was getting stuck with all kinds of tubes and my chest was on fire. I prayed God would let me live through this karma. I had so much I wanted to do. So much life I hadn't touched. He couldn't let me die just yet! I didn't give Ma a grandson to keep the King legacy going, you know? I still wanted to buy her a house out Maryland for her to retire in. I needed to know if Brandon was cool. I thought of Simone. I did a lot of things in life I wasn't too proud of. Where was I going? Heaven or Hell?

"Who the fuck is you talking to? I'm his mother!" Ma yelled out as she squeezed my right hand. I squeezed her back looking in her defeated eyes. Ma was a fighter and she was always in control, but this time she was helpless.

"If you want me to help, you have got to get out of my way," the lady shot back.

"Bitch you better help! He's still alive!" That was Ma. Always being extra. I was slipping in and out of consciousness but it couldn't have been more than a second later when I heard:

"If you want me to keep your son alive I need everybody out!" She yelled again with more assertiveness. I felt hands placing an oxygen mask over my face and then it was lights out again…

BRANDONS INTERLUDE

Two Weeks Prior

"Babe you know you can't be driving around without no license," Tina said trying not to cry as she prepared a big dinner for Brandon. She was trying to be the best woman for him that she could be but she just couldn't understand why he didn't want to leave the streets alone.

"Why you always telling me what I can and can't do like you my PO? Like damn get the fuck off my back bitch," he snapped popping one of the perc's she had been selling for him while he was locked up. He had a bottle of lean and took a sip as he frantically looked around the beat-up apartment. Brandon was tired of hearing Tina's mouth and decided to take the car and go for a spin but couldn't find the keys.

"I'm not babe…I'm just reminding you," she said trying to calm him down.

"Well I don't need you to remind me about shit Tina, damn! See this is why I need to go for a ride you getting on my fucking nerves with ya dumbass," Brandon yelled. He was getting angry because he couldn't remember where he put the keys at. He was trying to think back to when he got in the house that morning around 6am. His mind was too blurry which made him even more upset.

"Where the fuck is the keys Teen?" Brandon said calmly.

"I don't know baby you drove last," she said sliding the key out her bra and putting it under the toaster on the counter while he wasn't looking.

"Don't play with me La'Tina. Where the hell is the keys?" He said looking through all his pockets one more time.

"You don't need to be out there anyway, why don't you eat first?" she suggested.

"Bitch gimme the fucking keys!" He yelled now gripping her up by the throat. He shoved her into the wall next to the counter so

68

fast she didn't have time to think. Her eyes grew wide as his grip got tighter making her point to the toaster.

Brandon smacked the toaster off the counter revealing the key but made sure not to take his hand from around her neck. He punched the wall next to her then let her drop to the ground, grabbed the keys and leaned down in front of her.

"See, if you stop playing all the time I won't get so upset. Stop playing all the time. You know I'm stressed out trying to get my money back right. That way I can get my own car and you can be shopping and shit like before," he said trying to console her by rubbing her back.

"I don't want that stuff I just want you Bran," she cried.

"I'll be back," he said placing a kiss on top of her head.

Brandon walked outside and forgot where he was going so he took a drive to one of his old spots before he was locked up. It was a quiet block next to a playground around the corner from Tina's. He would go there to smoke, clear his mind and more than likely get some head from one of the girls who lived in the jects. In exchange he would give them a pill or let them smoke with him. If it was a good night he would get three young friends at one time who were looking for pills or weed. He happened to see one of his old whores, Trayanna, walking by this night in particular and rolled the window down.

"Wassup Tray Mama? Come smoke with me," he yelled to her.

The block was empty at that moment which was perfect for Trayanna. She didn't want to be caught being a hoe on a summer night and she definitely didn't want to run the risk of one of Flipp's people seeing her talking to the enemy. Flipp was a McCoy and hated Brandon. Trayanna knew Brandon always had free weed for his bitches and Flipp always charged full price whether you were his whore or not. She just got laid off that day for failing a random drug test and had no money so she figured Brandon would be her quick fix. Tray and Tina had been fighting over Brandon for years but it never failed. He always went back to Tina.

"Wassup B? Let's go for a ride," she said getting in the car. Trayanna felt it was finally her chance to have one up on Tina...

Brandon went against the code and took her to one of the stash houses in Olney so that he could grab some more pills. After that, he took her to get some ice cream and then down to Boathouse Row on Kelly Drive so they could roll up.

After a few puffs Trayanna started getting dizzy. She knew she was way too high for it to have been loud that they smoked and was ready to go but Brandon wasn't. She didn't know that when he stopped at the stash house he picked up some pills to sell since he used all of his. He grabbed a bag of weed and crushed up some Peak and laced the weed. When he rolled up by the river, she didn't even know Peak was in their blunt. She never tried the new drug before so it was making her feel dizzy. Trayanna knew the blunt was laced and fear consumed her.

Brandon remembered back to the last time they had sex before he was locked up and with all the lean, pills and weed he had that day he wasn't taking no for an answer.

"B chill out. I said I'm cool," she said now ready to go.

Brandon was being too pushy for her rubbing and squeezing her thighs trying to go up her oversized shirt she wore with latex shorts and a thin sports bra. She looked so he didn't care that she was scared.

"Nah, bitch! You smoke my shit, ask me for a ride and *now* you ready to go?" He said trying to remain calm.

"Look I'll pay you for it, just drive me home my wallet is in the house. I don't feel so good," Trayanna cried holding her head.

"You gonna let me fuck. Matter fact—get ya ass in the back," he said now holding his gun in plain sight so she could see. She tried to scream but the sound got caught in her throat. Besides, between the dark tint, the nearly empty parking lot and the Glock 9, she wasn't so sure anybody would hear her. She started reaching for the door and planning her escape when Brandon said:

"Aht, aht, aht…climb in the backseat," he said now cocking and waving the gun in her direction.

As Brandon forced his way inside of her raw, she began to cry and grimace at the pain. His sweat was all over her and she prayed he would be done quick. She kept telling him she couldn't breathe so he choked a little harder as he came inside of her. Brandon then climbed back into his front seat leaving her in the back alone to wipe herself with an old napkin she found on the floor.

"Get up front…I'll take you home," Brandon said.

Trayanna remembered she took her birth control which was a bitter sweet thought. What would it matter? She may not have been able to conceive that night but she would never get the stain out of her memory. She couldn't help but to think she was only going for a walk around the block to let off some steam about being laid off. She was happy to see Brandon because she remembered all the fun they had but knew she should have never got in the car with him. Rumor was he wasn't himself since he came home but she knew girls always gossiped and left it at that. As she sat in the passenger seat facing the window, she planned to tell Flipp what happened. She hated Tina for having B and now she wanted him dead for what he did to her. Two birds with one stone. She wanted to be alone for a few days and then she would start a war with those '*King niggas*', as Flipp would call them.

"Long night with the guys huh?" Tina asked quietly as Brandon slid under the covers holding her.

"Yeah…long night…" Brandon yawned before dozing off.

Tina could smell Trayanna's cheap perfume and decided not to say anything. A silent tear hit her pillow. Brandon seemed calm so instead of confronting him she stayed quiet. She didn't want to continue what happened in the kitchen before he left.

70

NINE

Y ou motherfucker!" D yelled out when I opened my eyes.
Everything was bright and I was squinting to see where I was.

"Stop cursing Delando," Ma said smiling and crying. She pressed the button for the nurse and gave me a big hug.

"Nigga we thought you was a goner! Who the fuck you think you is 50 or some shit? *'Many men, many many many many men, wish death upon me.'*" D rapped.

I tried to laugh but everything hurt. I could only smile.

"Man, you been down for 2 weeks! I gotta get some jokes in. Sorry for cursing Ms. K," D said laughing as he did a little dance around her.

I tried to move my left hand but I just felt throbbing. I lifted 2 fingers with my right hand as my way of asking—*two fucking weeks?!* I missed France. Then it finally hit me. Somebody tried to kill me dawg! I became angry and tried to take the tubes and wires out of me. I had to see where Brandon and Unc was. I had so many questions that my head started hurting.

"Sit back and wait for the nurse before you be out again dickhead!" D laughed.

"Delando that damn mouth of yours! Anyway, yes, my baby—two weeks. Oh God Brett you didn't leave me" Ma cried.

"Oh yeah. *Simooone* kept calling from ya job. I told her to give you a fucking minute. Ya job is too demanding for me personally. But hey you corporate cats love that shit. Oh sorry Ms. K." D said waving her off.

"Yeah she called crying." Ma said smacking D on the arm and wiping her tears. I knew she wanted to know more. She loved Uptown and I knew we would have a talk about it later because my doctor had just walked in. *Damn she called about me crying?*

"Hey Brett, I'm Dr. Reeves. It's nice to see you're up today. You were moving your right arm yesterday and you're looking around

72

today," he smiled while making notes on a chart. He was an older brown skin guy about Unc's age. He was a smooth looking dude with a salt and pepper lowcut and matching beard.

As Dr. Reeves ran some test over the next few hours, the nurses came behind him unhooking my breathing tube. Everyone was saying how good I was functioning for it to be my first day up. It felt like I just took a long ass nap.

The next day, I asked for D and Ma to stay in the room as Doc gave me the full run down. Basically because of all the blood I lost and how the bullet went through me busting my ribs, they had to operate on me. A piece of my rib cut into my heart. Ballistics came back confirming the bullet that hit me was from a .45 caliber gun. My body was going into shock and a blood clot formed and was on its way to my heart. Doc managed to locate the clot but I slipped into a coma.

"I believe in science, son. However, I do respect divine intervention. This is nothing short of a miracle. Your body was, essentially, shutting down. I guess as your mom puts it, God has a plan for your life. We have to keep you here to make sure everything goes well and monitor your hearts recovery. We also have to make sure you don't slip back into a coma. It looks like things can only go up from here if the Big Guy keeps doing my job for me," he said as he sent the nurses out.

"Now this is off the record," he continued. "I'm not sure what went down that night but your mom called in a favor being as though she doesn't care for Dr. Aaron." Ma told me how she didn't like the doctor that operated on me.

"However, she did a hell of a job operating on you and I assisted her. I had one of my old friends run the ballistics. Your friend D here said nothing with the police. Whoever did this was trying to kill you, son."

"How…ahem…do you know?" I asked.

"Well the way the first bullet hit you let me know you were the intended target. You were grazed on the left side of your head, son. Just a small graze only needing a bandage. It looks, to me, as if they went for your chest after the headshot but hit your shoulder then your left arm instead. Now," Doc said hanging up X-Rays, "this is where you were hit. Not a good shooter at all." I didn't even feel the shot in my head man. I was already drinking and smoking that night so I couldn't really remember.

"You talk to your mama. What are you into?" Ma sniffled.

"Nothing Ma. I'm…ahem ahem…I'm not into nothing," I said grimacing as I tried to move my left arm.

"That's bullshit Solomon!" She yelled out. I knew when she called me by my middle name she meant business. I looked at D for help but even he knew when and when not to try Karen 'Square Up' King.

"Kay relax, okay? The boy just woke up," Doc admonished. She calmed down and asked again what I was involved in. *Kay? Who the fuck is this dude?*

"Where's Uncle AJ and Brandon?" I asked now realizing they still hadn't come to see me.

"Who knows where those two idiots are," Ma spat throwing her hands up. She was holding her right hand to her temple while taking deep breaths. She always did that right before she beat me or Brandon growing up.

"D, I know it's getting late but can you try to get Simone for me? I need an update on France," I said ignoring everybody else. I needed to talk to Simone. She was going to have to be my muscle until I got back on my feet.

"Oh no, no, no. I already told Mary to cancel everything until Dr. Reeves says you can go back to work," Ma interrupted.

"Fuck no," I responded. Dukes was giving me a headache.

"Oh, hell nah! You wanna go back into a coma fool?!" She said walking towards me with a blank stare. Dr. Reeves grabbed her arm and pushed her lightly towards the door.

"Look that's enough. Brett, it's not advised that you start work right after you wake up from being in a coma. Just rest and let us—"

"Look Doc, I appreciate your help but I have business to handle. D can you please just tell Mone she should get here ASAP?" Fuck what they were talking about. D looked at my mom helplessly and let me know he would handle it for me.

Ma took a deep breath and said: "You're still not going anywhere so figure whatever it is you need to figure out from this bed, boy."

Dr. Reeves lingered back a little after we all said our goodbyes. He started saying if I needed help figuring out who hit me up to let him know so that he could help.

"Yeah and what do I owe for all these good deeds, my guy?" I asked annoyed.

"Ha…nothing, King. Just like Oliver. That's not a bad thing. But nope, nothing at all. Just want you to get healthy. Remember what I said. Happy your still here, son." Doc said walking out.

I really made it out alive. I remembered feeling like my life was slipping away from me in the middle of my club. Things got fuzzier and that white light was getting brighter and brighter. The last image I had was facing the entrance where I believed the shots came from. I had to get back on my feet. I needed to make sure my money was straight and I had to find out who tried to off me. I was more so concerned with the *why* part of it all.

74

TEN

The next day...

I had been seen by so many specialist, doctors and nurses that my head was spinning. I couldn't wait to get out of there and be around some familiar faces.

"Ya baby-mom here," D grinned.

"Huh?" I laughed.

"Coming down the hall in five...four...three...two—"

"Wassup Brett! Hey D. I was busy when D first called me but I returned your call as soon as I could," Simone smiled.

"Hey, Mone. You ain't take my place yet did you?" I joked.

"No not yet but if we had to choose between you and Simone, I'm picking baby girl every time," I heard Trevor say when Simone handed me her phone.

"I have everybody on the conference room phone for you," Simone whispered.

"Hey Brett this is your boss, Jon. You get your ass back here before you're fired, haha. No, Simone is doing an amazing job while you're gone. Good pick." I'm sure he winked when he said it. Jon pulled me in his office one day just to say it was nice having another cutie in the office besides Shayla.

"The King is risen," Trevor laughed. A young King was back huh? I had the keys.

"Don't scare me like that, child," Shayla chimed in.

"You sounding like Ma, Shay. Look guys, I'm still here and when I come back I'm coming for y'all jobs," I laughed.

Everyone else, including Ms. Mary, told me to get as much rest as I could and that they couldn't wait for me to get back. Jon told me he would call me in a few days and advised the rest of the crew to get back to work.

Simone said she had to make some phone calls so me and D kicked it until she came back. He let me know what was happening in the field and that everyone was holding things down. Unc thought it best to stay away from the hospital because he didn't want anyone to get any ideas.

D also let me know that he figured out my Uncle's longtime rival Tess McCoy had something to do with me getting hit. Tess was one of Flipp's four uncle's and was in charge of setting the hit up on me. Back in the day Unc called a truce with the McCoys but Flipp was always beefing with Brandon so the beef continued. What I wanted to know was why me?

By this time Simone was back and we switched up the conversation. Knowing I wanted some alone time with shorty, D said he had to get back to Dina and the kids and left.

Simone was quiet until the door was closed all the way. She walked slowly to my bedside and lightly hit me on my good arm with a laugh and tears in her eyes.

"Nigga if you would've checked out on me I was going to fuck you up." She tried to hide the tears by looking in her bag but I peeped. She was really getting emotional. It was hope for me.

"You get this emotional over all your managers?" I smiled yawning. My body was so tired and my pain meds were kicking in.

"I've never had a manager almost...you know," she said looking away. "Uh...anyway, the um, the Paris trip went really well. You would have been shocked watching me talking to *your* client...But after some serious negotiating with that girl Monique, who by the way was so upset you couldn't make the trip," she said with a side-eye, "we, well I, got the account," she smiled, showing some dimples I never paid attention too before. "I wanted to be the one to tell you."

I grinned hard as hell. God was really on my side man. I was about to get a crazy bonus. Monique was the wife and model to Edward Couture, a high-end fashion designer. They joined together and were running a high-end children's line and were pulling in crazy revenue. I had a thing or two with Monique when Edward was out of town on business but always managed to keep it professional. She came on to me when we were still in the beginning phase of the negotiating the deal. I know that's the reason I got the account and I don't know...I'm not proud of that. But I can say that this was my biggest account and I couldn't thank Simone enough for handling it for me.

"How you manage to close on it without me?"

"Je parle un peu de français," she winked.

"Bravo," I laughed.

"Merci monsieur King." Mone whispered. *Knowing Edward, it's no wonder we got the account.*

"Ahem...uh thanks for filling in for me Simone. I really appreciate it..." I said as she sat down in the chair next to my bed.

"I tried to come back in the club that night to check on you but D told me they had to rush you to the hospital. It was police all over the club...but the white girl, the bartender girl? She dropped me off at Char house and I think she drove here after that. I'm sure D told you I was calling," she said. "D has your car keys too and I think he parked your car at your crib but I'm sure he told you that too."

"Yeah he told me…thanks for being so concerned."

"I'm happy your up Brett. I was really nervous," she said staring off into space.

I reached my right hand out towards her. She looked at me for a few seconds then grabbed my pinky and ring finger. I fell asleep but when I woke up an hour later Simone was still there with her headphones in humming, still holding my hand with her eyes closed.

Out of every chick I ever fucked with, none of them ever made me so calm. Simone was gentle but confidant. Shit was attractive as hell and I ain't even hit that. I wasn't thinking about my family, hustling, work…not even the shooting. Just Mone, me and the hard ass hospital bed.

"Good, you're up," Simone said letting my hand go.

"Yeah, I'm sorry."

"No, you're okay Brett. Look, I have to get home but Jon gave me tomorrow off. If you want, I can come back to check on you?" She offered.

"Okay. Could you hang with me for a little while?" It was boring in there by myself. Mom and the gang were working and I was having flashbacks of the shooting. Company was always welcome.

"I think I can make that happen," she said before leaving.

"Visitation starts at 8:30—just saying." I replied.

"See you tomorrow Brett. Get some rest okay?" She leaned in and gave me a soft kiss on my cheek then left.

The rest of the night I tried to stay up by being on all my socials letting niggas know I was still around. Everybody was showing me mad love but I knew likes and comments didn't mean I really had support. I was down and was now becoming paranoid. To ease my mind, I kept replaying Simone's visit in my head as I dozed off.

ELEVEN

Hey Brett, your first visitor of the day is here bright and early."
Nurse Soeur said with a smile as she let Simone in. Soeur and
Schaeffer were the only nurses I wanted around. They were thorough
as hell with this nursing shit, so I ain't have to see too much of Dr.
Reeves.

Simone was sexy but on some chill type time this day I never
seen her this chill before and I liked it. She was wearing these jean
booty shorts, a plain hot pink spandex tank top with some black leather
thong sandals. Her hair was curly and sandy brown underneath a
LaShay graffiti wide brimmed hat. LaShay's was a local clothing line by
my homegirls Layah and Shaynice. I used to kick it with them back in
high school and whenever I ran into them it was love.

All the fly girls were rocking they line. They even had a little
following out Atlanta and Baltimore. It was high fashion with some
hood flavor. I loved seeing my folks' brands expanding and growing
and Simone was rocking it well. I made a mental note to link her up
with them hopefully as a local model. I was always thinking about
connections.

"Hey, Mone, you made it," I said happy to see her. When she
walked in, she had what looked to be a breakfast platter from Unc's
diner. My guy!

"Now you should NOT be eating these grits with everything
going on with ya heart and shit, but I know you could use some real
food," she said with that sneaky smile after my nurse left. Her eyes
were a little low under that hat too. I could tell she smoked. Wake and
bake! I was sick I wasn't going to be hitting no blunts any time soon.

She smacked my hand away when I reached for the turkey
bacon after she opened the platter.

"Nigga don't touch the meat,"

"Pause," I said snatching a piece anyway.

"Nigggaaaa, don't get me kicked outta here," she laughed.

She was right though I shouldn't have been eating any of that but I appreciated the life line.

"Simone...I'm going crazy in here you feel me?" I laughed.

"You ain't going crazy. I know you enjoying all ya fan mail." She nodded towards all the flowers and get-well cards I had and rolled her eyes.

"I think flowers are very thoughtful," I stated.

"Yeah okay. I'm sure one of your fans in here let you hit too."

"And what makes you think that?"

"You ain't see them joe ass bitches at the security desk *and* in the waiting-room. Rolling they eyes all hard when they realized I was coming to see you. Don't even get me started on that cookout you had awhile back," she said turning towards me slightly with a mouth full of grits. "I know somebody sweating you in here. I just don't know who."

"Yeah okay ain't nobody sweating me. I'm tryna sweat you but you playing." I responded. I saw she stopped eating. I didn't know if she was thinking of something smart to say or what but just as soon as she stopped she picked her spoon up again.

"Brett, you can't handle me."

"You what? 4'11? I think I can handle that."

"5'2 and a half actually and nope I don't think so. I know how you and all them niggas Shook be with operate. I don't play that monkey bullshit." She was right though. We were known to get bitches—that was just a fact.

"Just cause these whores," she continued, "doing whatever for a hoe badge—"

"A *hoe badge?*" I laughed.

"Yeah you know bragging rights for sucking y'all little dicks—"

"Ayoooo! Who said my dick was little?"

"Don't tell me you talking Shrimpanese, King." *She look sad, ha.*

"Simone stop playing aight?" *My shit ain't little, fuck she thought.*

"Anyway. Y'all the get money guys. Beard Gang I think is y'all name. These girls are willing to do anything to get y'all and y'all love it. You can't handle me cause you still playing games. You don't even know how to be by yourself how you gonna seriously be with me?" she laughed turning back around. It was a sarcastic 'I won' laugh and I found her more attractive. *Women.*

I posted a throwback Thursday pic on the Gram from the night Simone came through to happy hour. I was sitting in between her and Shayla and they were both leaning towards me cracking up. We were all laughing at something funny Trevor said as he took the picture. I wrote how I couldn't wait to be back in the swing with them. Dr. Reeves said one more week. I think Mom was making him keep me there longer than needed, but it was all good.

"I fuck with you" I said out of nowhere. Mone locked her phone and gave me her undivided attention.

"Do I find you attractive? You damn right. Not just physically though. You on ya shit Mone. I really fuck with you…I'm telling you I can handle you," I challenged. Silence.

"Take your hat off." I said quietly. As she did, I couldn't help but notice that she was blushing. She had a different pair of glasses on this day. I liked these ones. They were black Ray Bans and not as gaudy as the gold frames she wore. I took her glasses off and stared at her. She had these deep pretty almond shaped brown eyes and her eyelashes were long and thick. Her eyebrows were natural looking enough. You could tell she had a little make up on but not as much as some chicks I knew. It was too hot to be all caked up. Mone had round cheeks and full brown lips. Like Susie Carmichael. She had a mole on her right cheek and these cute dimples. Her skin was a copper colored brown. Like a shiny penny—from head to toe. She was looking good and I pictured her having my kids. It was a weird thought that I never saw with nobody other than Uptown at one point. I knew that feeling and it made me look at her differently. In a good way though. She looked older and sexier and I was loving it.

"What you thinking about, Boss Baby?"

"I want you but you playing these games. I be seeing you checking me out at work and shit. Let's get this money together. Let's grind and make these niggas and bitches jealous together. I'm tryna wife you ma," I blurted out. My boys would KILL me hearing me say that kind of stuff.

"Brett you just talking…you laid up in this hospital bed going half-crazy, looking at these bum ass bitches and you just talking," she responded waving me off again.

"These bum ass bitches huh?"

"Seriously Brett…we work together. I told you before I don't fuck my bosses."

"Shit, Jon bouta give you my job anyway. Can you hire me as your assistant? Then it won't be an issue" I said making her laugh.

"You just got all the jokes today," she said still smiling.

"Simone I'm forreal,"

"I know Brett…what about your groupies?"

"Come on baby that shit irrelevant wassup with us? It ain't gonna affect work or no shit like that. You a boss. You know how to keep it professional when needed, right?" I questioned. I wasn't used to working like this for no chick. Old and young alike.

"It's not about keeping it professional, boo. It's about being real and realistically speaking this wouldn't work," she said.

"So then why you here with me on your day off at almost 9 in the morning?" I genuinely asked. Silence again.

"Sassy Simone don't have no comebacks?" I laughed when that made her suck her teeth. She always had a comeback for me. It was nice having the last word on that one. As I grabbed my phone again to check my texts.

My Queen: Hey baby boy. I'm stopping by.
Me: When?

"Want me to go?" Simone said standing up with an attitude.

"Sit ya short ass down you ain't going nowhere," I laughed.

"Fuck you King."

"You promise?"

"Promise what?" Ma said busting in.

"Hey wassup, Ma. You remember Simone from the cookout?"

"Hey Ms. Karen," Simone smiled sitting back down.

"Hey Baby Boy." Ma straight up ignored Mone.

"Oh okay," Simone smirked. I could tell she was feeling a way but she would learn—that was just Ma for you.

"Stacy, do you mind if I have a word with *my* son?"

"*Suuure.* Boo I'll be back. *Simone's* going to go get you some ice," Mone grinned kissing me on the cheek. I peeped her roll her eyes as she walked out my room. It was all amusing to me.

"I will drag that little tramp up outta here by her weave if she pulls a stunt like that again. Got her ass all out. So that's what took you so long to text me back? Better be glad she's Mary's niece! *Grits?!*" She snapped looking at the window seal. "I know that hussy ain't give you no damn grits! How old is she?" *Oh lord.*

"Ma can you chill? That was her breakfast," *Not today.* This day was supposed to be about me and Simone. Not Ma.

"Look I'm going to be cordial with your little friend. I'm not staying long anyway. I just came by to see you before I run some errands. Are you happy you're almost out of here?" She said watering my flowers and opening up the blinds.

"Thanks Ma. Yeah, I am. I'm just ready to get back to life as normal, you know?" I responded.

"Don't go rushing anything, baby. People be hating and whoever did this knows who you are and where you be. Nothing wrong with laying low for a minute. You follow the doctor's orders and stop all that smoking and drinking." She said.

We talked for a few minutes longer. She let me know that she talked to Brandon. Mom was usually against violence but I was baby boy and she was just ready to get back to life as normal. That's why she told him to handle whoever did it and to keep us out of it. Little did she know I was already in this too deep.

"Well I'm going to leave you two alone—don't want to interrupt anything," Ma said in a forced sweet tone a few minutes after Simone came back. I peeped Simone roll her eyes again but I ain't mention it. Ma could be a pain.

Simone kicked it with me until visitor hours were over. I honestly appreciated the company and kept thanking her all day for it. We watched movies, cracked jokes and got turned up on the livestream I made for Shook's music. She was really becoming a good friend...

"Well Brett, I'm going to get ready to go," she yawned.

"Gotta get back to ya boo huh?" I joked.

"Ehh...I gotta get home let's leave it at that." She replied getting her stuff ready to go. It was hard watching her leave. Harder than I thought it would be.

"Can I get a kiss?" I asked jokingly.

She looked at me sideways, walked towards me and gave me a sweet, soft and slow kiss.

"I was playing but I could use one more," I laughed.

"You have a good night Brett," she winked as she walked out.

Damn. Simone really fucked with me. I fucked with her too and was willing to do whatever it took to get her. She called to let me know she got home safe and then I drifted off to sleep.

SIMONE'S INTERLUDE

I-95 North...

Simone just left from seeing Brett and was trying to make it home to finish working on her style blog. From the creative side to the logistics, it was all she could think about lately besides her new love interest and work. Being hired at New Enterprises was the best thing that could have happened for her during this time. Finally, something legal was funding her business venture. She was getting some of the best marketing experience; Brett and Shayla really took her under their wing and she was soaking all of her newfound knowledge up like a sponge. Simone knew in a few years she could leave the corporate life for good and become the entrepreneur she always wanted to be.

Simone turned down Vine Street to get on 95 when she decided to hit her homegirl up.

"Char Baby. Wassup?"

"Girl I have been calling you all day and you just now picking up? Aht aht. Where you been? I was trying to have some girl time while the weather is still nice. Get some crabs and have a picnic down Kelly Drive or something," Char said sounding neglected.

Brett connected Shook with some local music producers and with the way his buzz was growing, he didn't have much time for Char. He always made it clear she was the one though. *'Can't make money and give you all my time,'* was what he told her. Of course, he admitted he learned that idea from Brett. Just a few months had passed since the cookout and the two were messing with each other heavy.

Char was dramatic and at times could be clingy when her men weren't acting right but Simone didn't mind. *This girl needs an academy award,* she thought to herself smiling. "I saw your call boo. I had some stuff to take care of that's all," she told her friend.

"Oh, for the blog?" Char cheerfully replied.

"No girl. Let me tell you...I went to see Brett." Before she could continue, Charmaine was already on it like she was there.

"Okay so more than likely you smoked cause you're a pothead for real and then went up there to give Brett some hospital pussy! You nasty!" she said cracking up.

"Bitch please! First of all, I'm not a pothead. I told you it's my detox medicine," Simone laughed. "Second, I ain't giving him no pussy…yet," she said making Char scream.

"Biiitch! You crazy as hell. I just know them bitches was in there hating too! Same ones posting him up doing no face no trace. I hate when bitches do that. tryna act like they wit somebody and Brett don't care if they cover his face or not. You the only one I ever seen him post on his page. Girl I don't know how you do it…" Char rambled on.

Simone knew her girl was right though. Brett was the guy to have. Everybody—girls and guys alike—were trying to be connected to him and his friends. Everyone was in love with the myth of the King family and how they were worth millions. She didn't know if she believed all the rumors like her girlfriend though. How could a drug family in the city's hostile drug and policed environment, still be making money on the scale that many believed? Simone just didn't think it was possible. Brett and his boys were into music and entertainment, so it was a possibility, but she just didn't see Brett as a drug dealer. He was too cheesy to sell drugs in her mind but Char sipped the drug dealer myth juice.

Simone really didn't care who was posting Brett on their page and who was liking or screenshotting what. Who-shot-who-because-somebody's-baby mama's-cousins-brother-snitched, just didn't excite her. No matter what though, Simone always entertained her homegirls gossip. Char was all for knowing the tea. It wasn't always a bad thing either. She knew everybody and always had the latest scoop which sometimes worked in Simone's favor.

"Yeah you right these bitches irritating for real," Simone said debating what she wanted for dinner.

"Yes, they are. Enough about all that though spill the tea bitch what happened with Brett," Char laughed.

"Oh. My. Goodness. Char he is so sweet and he knows exactly what to say. He is smooth as fuck—I will give him that but he on some other type time," she said hesitantly. She didn't want to go into too many details because she was still soaking up the day but she also wanted to share her pent-up excitement.

"What you mean 'other type time?'" Char questioned nosily.

"He wants to be in a relationship. Like, he wants to be my dude or whatever and I just don't know how to feel about that. He's so damn fine but I just don't want to deal with him at work and at home. Been there done that and I'm not tryna do it again," she confessed.

Her last failed relationship started off with her and her ex Travis being coworkers at a department store and it was suffocating.

Day in and day out she was around the same person making him become obsessed with her. If a male customer even looked her way he would blow up at her. Outside of work Trav was emotionally abusive and soon became physically abusive as well. Simone needed her freedom. If she wanted to get away she had to sneak which caused Trave to become even more insecure and believe she was cheating. For Simone could hear her late mother saying: *too much of anything was a bad thing baby.*

"Well you can't compare the two Monie. Brett is name brand and Travis is generic to me. Plus, that sounds like an excuse. Girl *thee* Brett King wants you to be his girl. *Mr. Player for Life* is ready to settle down and let you upgrade him but you comparing him to your corny ass ex? Mr. Broke himself? Bul was an insecure ass pussy. He was always mad when we tried to go out and have fun, talked to you like you was a basic bum bitch, tried to isolate you from your family and friends, made you turn down job opportunities because he was scared you would meet someone better, AND he *tried* to fight Brett for being nice that day Travis wouldn't come get you in the rain then had the nerve to get knocked out then beat on you for the rest of the night. We tryna be fuck-boy free remember?" Char reminded her girl getting mad all over again. Simone laughed and silently thanked her friend for feeling some anger for her. Simone didn't have the energy to really take it in that a man she loved and hated for years was finally out of her life. It was scary and refreshing.

"Well, yeah…I don't have to answer to nobody though Char. I finally got my new place…it's peaceful and quiet. Shit, not shaving—"

"Oh, aht aht hoe I was with you 'til the 'no shaving' part. At least wax. I can hook you up with my girl who owns a wax place in Manayunk, shit," Char laughed.

"Text it to me, ha. No, but seriously, Sis I'm loving this new freedom I have and I don't know if I want to be tied down just yet," Simone replied seriously.

"Girl cuffing season is approaching. You better get your mind right. Besides, love isn't bondage—it's freedom that you create with another person," Char stated. Char knew how powerful the two together could be. She thought back to the car ride home after Brett's cookout.

Simone was so upset about Maya being there. Char was too. Char understood her friend's irritation though. She was tired of the hating hoes staring at her all night but as always, Simone kept her cool and continued to enjoy herself and all the attention Brett was giving her. From Char's perspective, Maya was looking desperate for Brett to pay her some mind that whole night and Ms. Karen was being a little too joe. It didn't seem that Brett really wanted Maya there and that's what Char and the twins let Simone know.

Char did her digging as always and figured out Maya and Brett weren't even dealing with each other anymore at that time. But the cookout put some doubt in Simone's mind making her stick around a little longer with Travis. Char was so happy when they finally split ways a week prior, she could have thrown a party. Her friend was finally free.

Char never paid Brett any attention in a flirtatious way but what she did like about him was the way he looked at Mone when they were together. He was also very chill and laid back the way Simone liked her men. Plus, he was about his money and very respectful. Char could appreciate any stand-up dude who was getting paid and was about his community. Char knew Brett was the missing puzzle piece in Simone's life. Now, Char didn't like to pride herself as a match maker but she did have a record of linking people up. Some were even married! She didn't want her sister-friend to pass this soul by.

"Char you funny as shit," Simone laughed.

"You laughing but I'm serious. I think Brett really likes you. He has a legitimate job, no kids, and he only want you. I don't see the problem. But back to the story. What happened next?"

As Simone let her girl know all the juicy details of her day, she began to self-reflect and started realizing she was smiling hard. She just left the drive thru of her favorite burger spot. In between bites of her fries she said: "A bitch is cheesing like shit, I'm *scared*."

"What you scared of crazy girl?" Char asked.

"He is the type of dude to have you all stupid and you didn't even get the dick yet. Damn! He's bringing out the sucker in me already. You don't need that kind of dick in ya life, Monie Girl…It's not healthy" Simone said talking to herself.

"I have not seen you act this crazy over no nigga since that time Ray Hamilton kissed you in front of the whole class in the second grade. Ya chocolate ass was blushing so bad and almost ran into the door trying to get out of there."

"Ooooo you bitch! You know I tried to forget about that shit. I was so embarrassed oh my gosh. Friend, seriously though…King makes me giddy as fuck from just talking about dumb shit like work. Like what the fuck," Simone said feeling defeated.

She didn't want to be another flavor of the week for Brett. She heard all of the rumors about him and his many women—young and old. She couldn't lie though. Brett was irresistible to her. Even when she was with Trav, Brett was always in the back of her mind for some reason. She never thought about another man when she was with Travis until she met Brett. Maybe, just maybe, she thought to herself— Brett beating up Travis put the icing on the cake for her.

"So, what you gonna do because I know you and you're only going to go but so long without the D," Char joked.

"I'm celibate."

"Yeah okay bitch. I'm done with you. Seriously though, don't just chalk it. Really think about what Brett was saying to you. Just give it some thought," Char said trying to convince her to live a little.

"Why you going so hard?" Simone questioned. She knew her girl but shit, dick was the main reason many women she knew hated each other. The drought of good men—let Char and the media tell it— turned friend to foe.

"Trust me Shook hitting this thing just right," Char moaned making Simone laugh some more. They were girls, practically sisters. Char could respect Mone for asking her and she was happy to give her the honest truth. She wanted nothing but the best for her friend.

"No real shit though. I just like the way Brett fuck with you. Just be open minded is all I'm saying."

"Yeah you right. Ard girlfriend I'm walking in the house now and I don't want the twins to hear me coming in. I'm gonna text you."

"Ard sis."

Simone took a long shower as soon as she walked in the door. She worked on her blog for a little bit but after 30 minutes she couldn't even concentrate. After debating with herself whether to call or text, Brett, she heard Char's voice telling her to live a little.

"Hey King. I'm home."

"Okay cool…look I wasn't tryna pressure you earlier I'm just serious about you shorty," Brett yawned into the phone. His groggy voice did something to Simone. *What the hell*, she thought to herself, *I see why the hoes always on him, everything he does is so sexy.*

"Oh yeah?" She responded shyly.

"Yeah. I think you want me just like I want you. Matter of fact—I know you do but for some reason you being all hesitant about it…but I'm a patient dude, Monie Love."

"I know you are…look maybe we can just start off slow. I just got out of a relationship and I want to get to know you first. I want to be your friend," she said nervously. She worked with him every day and still got butterflies.

"Are you asking me to be besties?" Brett laughed. He noted her school girl behavior but he didn't get annoyed like normal. He hated games but knew she wasn't trying to play any games. She was just nervous about the idea of them being together. He *was* a King, right?

"Yes…I guess I am. Be my best friend and then we can see about being lovers," she said shocking herself. She was so awkward with men but Brett made her feel secure and protected.

"I can get with that Mone." he yawned.

"Good night, King."

"Good night, Bestie. I'll call you tomorrow. Hang up first."

"Um…what if…what if I don't want to just yet?"

"Stay on til I'm sleep then. How 'bout that?" yawned again.

"Deal."

Simone got comfortable in her bed and turned the T.V down just enough to hear but not enough to make out any sounds. She couldn't believe she was acting like a teenager. Scary—but she liked it. She grabbed her bonnet, said a little silent prayer that she didn't fall too hard too fast, and fell asleep to the sound of Brett breathing.

TWELVE

One month later...

O kay Brett and Simone, I talked to Jon long and hard about collaborating with y'all two so I need y'all on y'all shit, okay?" Shayla said putting her glasses on getting right to business.

It was the end of the third quarter and everybody knew what that meant. Crunch time. Audits, contract renewals, meetings...As hectic as it was I loved it. Besides nothing was better than Friday afternoon meetings meaning we could leave early and I could go kick it with the gang.

"Listen this is the time everybody bids on each other's accounts. It gets cut throat but it's just business. Look at how each exec could have closed a better deal, reach out to the marketing and sales reps to strategize and make sure your audits are spotless. Now why won't this thing ever work for me..." Shayla mumbled to herself.

She was trying to pull up the projector screen from her laptop but it wasn't working. As young and hip as she was, technology was never her thing. The projector came out of the middle of the wooden conference room table but kept going up and down making me laugh.

"Oh, shut it Brett. Help me out now, shit." she said exasperated. Before I could move she finally got it to work, making her do a little dance, then she hit the lights. It was now dim in the conference room and I caught Simone smiling and winking at me.

Mone finally came around after I got shot and became my homegirl for real. She still ain't let me hit and I was going crazy but I didn't care how long it took—I was going to get this girl to be my wife. I had some secret bitches on the side so it wasn't about nothing. Nah, she wasn't my girl but I needed her to see it was all eyes on her. A man has to be a man though, you feel me? We had so many rumors swirling around the city about us. You would catch us at a pro basketball game, chilling at her nephew's little league baseball practice, going to get some water ice and cheese pretzels on 33rd and Cecil B. Moore...You might catch us chilling down by the water at the hammocks on Christopher

Columbus Boulevard, and more than likely you could always catch us at her favorite restaurant on 15th and Chestnut Street downtown. Happy hour was always the move for us. Whatever she was in the mood for— if I had time—we were doing it. I was really courting this girl and I had to admit, it wasn't so bad.

"Now, if you two follow my lead-Chinese Santa is giving out Christmas bonuses," Shayla said laughing to herself. Jon was a cool boss and he was all about his money. Work hard? You got paid.

Trevor and all the guys felt Jon was playing favorites but Shayla was just a step faster and always showed up ready to eat. She was a natural hustler born and raised in West Philly in an area known as The Bottom. That was more than enough for her to finesse Jon and get us on her team before the guys even had time to plan.

When I got cleared to come back to work a few weeks after I was shot, Jon got right down to business. He told me at our monthly meeting that he was consolidating workloads for the next fiscal year and creating teams due to travel expenses. So, my training position that I didn't even get to operate in for a full year, was gone just as quick as it came. Shayla was my new captain. We just locked in a few different accounts but still Jon was cutting back. It didn't make sense to me but I didn't say too much. With everything I had going on with Brandon and Unc, I didn't even care.

"Now since most of our clients are in the same locations in the US we'll be working together on these accounts," Shay said flipping through her slide show.

"Jon said you'll see no pay cuts. It's been a long year in the making of this dream team I created so please y'all, *please*, don't make me look bad. Since we're consolidating, Simone, you'll be working at full capacity like the rest of us. I think it's too soon but you got this girlfriend," Shayla assured her.

"Sorry Brett, that means we need all hands-on deck. All correspondence needs to be sent directly to me." She knew I was trying to have less work and felt bad my job got phased out so fast.

"I just have to think smart about how to keep the money rolling, our clients happy, and our work life balance. I hate when prices rise…Well, anyway, we are trying to generate more revenue so we're going to be hitting up the big dogs. We're going to be making a lot of appearances with some pretty well to do folks so no drama please," she said not looking away from her notes.

"Okay Simone, did you finish the budget review?" she asked.

"Of course, Lady," Mone replied sliding the portfolio across the table to Shay.

"Well damn heifer. This whole time I thought I was thorough. Very clear and concise. You're keeping up great Monie," Shayla smiled as she and Mone dissected her budget.

"I love a smart girl on my team, no offense Brett," Shayla giggled. I was setting up some sales with Eddy's guy out Limerick so I wasn't paying her too much attention when she said my name again.

"Okay, see—Mone ain't who I'm worried about it's you and that damn phone, Brett," Shayla said rolling her eyes at me while pointing her red clicker my way.

"I need all focus and all hands-on deck," she said enthusiastically. "I've been working hard and mama need some new red bottoms. Everybody should've read their emails. Y'all bonus numbers looking good? Speak now or keep it pushing." Me and Simone nodded in agreement that we were cool.

"Okay good. So, me and Trevor were talking. As much as I wanted to say no, he convinced me that this move would be better in the long run. He's willing to let go of the new Ramirez account if we let go of Depressio and Gonzalez," She said smiling. As I started looking at the screen, I could see why she was willing to give up two accounts for one. Ramirez was balling and his new travel agency based in Mexico was gaining a lot of attention.

"Ramirez?" Simone asked as she looked through his file.

"Yes, is there a problem?" Shayla peered over her glasses.

"Not at all. I've just heard so much about him. He's like a self-made millionaire from Mexico and he did it in like three months. Business goals for real," Simone said putting her coffee down and passing the file back to Shayla. That made me sit up.

"I see somebody did their research. Good. Now that you guys are going to be handling this type of account I have to trust that you both will be on top of everything. This could mean big things for us…" Shayla went on. I sent the name to Eddy and told him to find out as much information as he could for me. He said he would get back to me and that he was swamped already. I ain't want to hear all that but I said okay.

While the ladies bounced ideas off of each other on how to get everything underway I tuned them out. I was checking with Brandon making sure that our guys were ready for our regular monthly shipment. With the help of Eddy, we were staying cool and off of Philly PD's radar. Eddy had some dirty undercovers as his lookouts. Man, it felt good. I couldn't stand the pigs and getting over without them being smart enough to know felt really good. It was like we were invincible…I was about to see my first million dollars and no one even knew. Shit no one could even tell. The boys were calling me Ace to poke fun at how chill I was. Always smooth but never extra. I was ready to leave this corporate world behind and start my own record label with my newfound riches. Shook would be my very first artist, of course.

While detailing what I needed for my business plan, I didn't even hear Shayla say we were taking lunch. I had to check out a new crib I was looking to rent so I decided to check it out on my break. I made my way to the luxury apartments just a few blocks north from my job's suite on 17th and Chestnut. Simone wanted to come with me but I convinced her it would be a quick trip. It was my spot but she gave me some good ideas as far as what to look for so I knew she wanted to see what I found. Ma always decorated my cribs but this time around I let Simone have some say.

As I walked to the apartments I thought about how my life was appearing to be so normal and plain but really it was stressful and I was starting to become more and more paranoid. Every dark tinted car made me tense. Any hood dude I ran across who stared too long made me want to grab my gun. I wanted to tell Simone what was going on since she had a unique way of calming me with her words but Unc always told me to keep the women out of the business. It always ended in disaster. I wondered how he knew but as long as he was hustling, I'm sure he had his fair share of bullshit.

The only thing that was keeping us under the radar was the fact that we weren't your average drug dealers. We didn't stand on the corner all day or chill on somebody's stoop all night. We were the working class and had money makers and other working-class folks as customers. Eventually we stopped selling individual pills and only responded to bulk order request. No less than 20 pills per order. The money was rolling in quick! We already re-upped twice since the first batch thanks to having Eddy's bul doing some of the work for us.

On top of that, Brandon had been smoking heavy since he'd been home. He was fucking his PO so she never tested his urine. Rumor had it he was taking Peak when no one was around. He was my own brother but I wasn't recognizing him anymore. He was getting ruthless and sloppy. Big dinner parties, renting out hotel floors and suites, driving shit that wasn't allowed in the city, and getting his young-boys to trash anybody who came at him or his bitches wrong. As terrible as he treated his women—nobody else was allowed to disrespect them. Crazy right? Brandon was trying to get his life on track but the fast money was eating him alive. I needed to talk to Unc about him and I had to do it quick.

I didn't see any of the guys as snitches. But I knew it was only a matter of time before somebody got the take-over bug, started hating or tried to plan a coupe. In my mind it was inevitable. I couldn't help but to feel that the cops were either planning a quiet attack or that they were dumber than I imagined. I was still feeling conflicted about everything I was doing but as Brandon always assured the team 'it's just business.' Leave it up to Brandon and we would all end up facing life with no parole messing around with him.

Flipp and his uncle Tess obviously got word that me and Brandon was flooding the streets with pills on a level they had never seen. All I could do was get taken back to the summer when I caught my first body. I knew other sets would get word that me and Brandon had the hood rockin' and would be popping up trying to join us or take us out sooner or later. The McCoy's had problems with Unc for as long as I could remember so it was only a matter of time before somebody threatened what we had going on.

As always, I made sure Eddy was on top of things but even he was getting nervous about his affiliation with us. He called me that previous night and let me know how serious he was.

"Look dude, your brother is spending WAY too much. Why can't he be regular like everybody else? No offense, but there's no way a dude from the hood just got out of jail and is balling already from working at a tire shop. I'm not worried about cops. I'm worried about other dealers coming for us. Talk to your brother before he fucks it up for everybody." He warned.

Eddy was white and understood the odds we were up against. He would go down and get probation and a lesser sentence than us…the rest of us were looking at *years*—maybe life if we got caught. The life of a hustler. It was a gamble and Unc always let me know that discretion was one way to avoid trouble.

***

"So, what about my floor in the bedroom closet? I want to be able to press a button and the middle of that shit pops up. Like a safety deposit box," I stated looking around the spacious suite.

When Tanesha (my realtor) let me know she had a better spot than the one I sent her from a few blocks away, I didn't believe her. But, as always, she came through. It was the perfect spot for me. From my view I could see the whole city! The Blu Chateau was the hotspot for all the ballers. From big name CEO's in the penthouse to the rookie ball players. It was just what I expected. Personal garage, valet parking, private swimming pools and hot tubs. A meeting hall, dry cleaners, workout room and a bar. Even though it was four stacks per month (which was already being discounted for me thanks to Neesha being the property managers niece) I had no complaints. One day I would get another home but for now I needed this kind of living.

I ain't want nobody to know where my new spot was so I asked Shook to move into my crib on Greene Street and take care of Blue for me. Ma bought the house for me before it got torn down and had D fix it up. That house was my baby but I needed to get out the hood where I could see things a little clearer. I still needed eyes and ears in that neighborhood and Shook was begging to get put on to the game we had. I told him no drugs were to be sold there but to just hold the spot down. He was already dying to get out of his grandma's house so for $500 a month it was his. Little did he know the five he was paying me was going towards his contract as my first artist. I wasn't trying to scam on him. He was a brother and I wanted him to be set and have faith in me as a boss, mentor and friend.

"I'm sure we can talk with management and work the safety deposit thing out baby boy, let me call them now," Neesha said snapping me back.

Neesha was the baddest in the real estate business and she was also fine as hell. She was a very petite Blasian girl with a nice little frame, pretty long hair and wore nothing but top designers. Mainly boutiques in the city but she always had her red bottoms on. She used to play me in undergrad but recently, once she saw I was the top guy in my city, she was giving me all the attention. Neesha knew I was getting more and more serious with Mone and didn't like the distance she was sensing from me.

"Yeah if I can get that safe? You got my bread for this deal. Very nice," I said now looking around the kitchen while she crunched numbers. It was the best suite I'd seen in a while. Long windows with remote controlled blinds showed the best view of the city. I could see the sunrise in my bedroom and the sunset in the living room. Brand new marble countertops, stainless steel appliances and a balcony with a built-in fire pit sealed the deal for me. Neesha spoke with management and confirmed we could do whatever we liked to the place. They figured my idea added to the suite so for an extra stack onto my security deposit they would make it happen.

"I got you a damn good deal and it's close to your job. You're welcome" Neesha smiled shaking my hand.

We talked a little business and I let her know I was planning to move in within the week. We went out to the balcony to just catch up on old times while I had a few minutes.

"We used to have fun Brett, what happened?" Neesha asked.

"You know. People change. Work started getting busy...you'll always be special to me Neesh, you know that," I said looking at her.

"How special?" She asked biting her lip.

Next thing I know I'm kissing on her and pulling up her dress. The balcony was secluded enough so I sat her on the ledge holding onto the small of her back. I slid a condom on that was in my wallet and worked my way inside as she wrapped her legs around me. It still hit like I remembered. Me and Neesha's sex was always crazy. I missed it and I was caught up in the moment. After we fixed ourselves and got ready to go, I noticed my phone had two missed calls from Simone. I told Neesha we would talk and that I had to get back to the office. I signed the lease agreement and let her do what I paid her to do.

On my way out, I could see a black car with tints across the street. I kept walking and the car finally pulled off. I didn't know why but like I mentioned before, it made me feel tense. I shrugged it off and made my way back to the office.

THIRTEEN

One week later...

It was a Saturday afternoon and I hadn't really heard from Simone. We would talk at work but after that she got ghost on me. We had been playing this courting game for some time now and I was ready to lock shorty in.

Me: I'm outside
Simone: Why you popping up uninvited?
Me: You don't want to see me?
Simone: Not at all
Me: Now if I go back home...

I was twenty minutes away so that gave her some time to respond after I saw she read my message. I waited another ten minutes outside her crib. Still no reply. Right when I was about to pull off I got a response:

Simone: 3B. Lock the front door behind u pussy

Oh yeah, she big mad, I thought to myself.

I was at the studio with D and Shook before I headed to shorty house. I asked him to hold it down and told him I would hit him up later. D laughed knowing where I was about to go but didn't press. We had a talk about her getting ghost on me and in D's infinite macking wisdom, he advised I show her who Big Daddy was, ya feel me? I wanted Simone to know I was serious. She asked me to come kick it with her for the day a week before but I got caught up with the guys at this rave selling pills until like four in the morning. I figured that's why she was mad. *Women hold grudges forever.*

I circled back around the block and found a shady spot underneath a couple of trees. I tucked my gun on my waist, put my

Flyers cap on, looked in the window one good time to brush my beard and walked down the block to her crib. Mone finally grabbed her own spot right off Roosevelt Blvd. & Bustleton Ave. It was this big three-story house that was turned into three apartments and of course she had the top floor. I got to her front door and turned the knob.

I locked up after walking in and smelled some good food cooking around a little hallway. I looked around at some pictures as I followed the scent. She was a cute kid. Thankfully she looked exactly the same since what looked like middle school. I saw prom and homecoming queen pictures. Sweet sixteen and college send-off party photos were hanging up too. She seemed like she was always thorough. It was a cute little apartment. You could tell a woman decorated it but it was chill enough for a dude to live there too. I stopped at a picture of her, the twins and her ex. They looked young and pretty happy.

"RUFF! RUFF! RUFF!"

I heard her dog, a brown and black Akita, running towards me with light footsteps not too far behind him. "Fuck him up Boss!" Simone laughed as he growled while trying to bite my ankles.

"Really Simone? If you don't get ya fucking dog I'm-a feed him to my Pit," I laughed kicking him off me.

"Yeah whatever Boss ain't no bitch. Ain't that right Bossy," she said in baby talk making him wag his tail.

"Boss, floss, Rick Ross—he still can't beat Blue," I scoffed.

"Keep talking shit Brett…you're already on thin ice. Sneakers off please," she said rolling her eyes and walking into the kitchen. I did as I was told and then made my way to the kitchen. Boss was standing in front of her watching me with his head cocked to the side.

"Sit boo," she said and immediately he sat down rubbing her foot with his nose.

"Ain't y'all cute," I smiled walking up behind her. I wrapped my arms around her waist and dug my nose into her neck. She stopped stirring some red sauce and leaned her head back. We stood like that for a minute until she gently pushed me off and started preparing some noodles for what looked like lasagna. My favorite.

"How you know I like lasagna?"

"A little birdy told me," she winked. *Shayla.*

"So, you a chef too, huh?" I asked jokingly.

"I can cook very well. Maybe if you act right I'll give you some. Want something to drink?" she said bending over to grab a pan out of her sidebar in the dining room. I declined the drink and let her know I liked how she hooked her place up. Her home was decorated nicely. It was kind of retro with splashes of green and blue. Stainless steel appliances and funky disco rugs were all over the medium sized apartment. On the walls were abstract paintings and some black art she mentioned she got from a local artist. I liked her style.

97

"I thought you lived with ya people?" I asked. When she first moved she said she would be staying with the twins.

"Yeah they live in the other two apartments downstairs. The property manager said he was starting fresh and kicked all his old tenants out. Of course I had to look out for my babies. They always in here though. I just would like a little more space that's why I'm saving up for a nice little condo and in a few years, I'm moving." She said smiling hard.

"I'm moving to something kind-a like a condo," I offered.

"I ain't living in ya whore house, you gotta buy me something nice" she said turning around smiling at me. "I'm getting out of the city. Maybe King of Prussia or Plymouth Meeting. Something else..."

Mone looked like she had just got out the shower. Her hair was curly and smelled like shampoo or something. She had this nice smelling spray on and was barefoot. She wore some little black Nike shorts and a purple dry-fit sweatshirt with no bra that hung off her shoulders and was cut to show her stomach. Simple and sexy.

"Why you look like you want me to strip?" She blushed.

"Because I do."

She laughed and started cleaning up.

"Why you come over here?" She asked not looking at me.

"I wanted to see you away from work and everybody. Just us."

"Why today? Why not last week when I asked you?" She was hurt that I bailed on her. That was a first for me. I was spoiling her with my time and didn't know how to stop.

"I got a lot going on that I'd rather you not see so sometimes I gotta lay low mama," I answered.

"That's bullshit. Why not just tell me everything up front? You can tell me that you fuck with me but want to see other bitches," She was staring me down with her arms crossed.

"I can't tell you everything baby and stop assuming. I wasn't with no bitches last Saturday," I replied honestly.

"I'm not ya baby Brett." *Ice cold.*

"Eh, not yet. But what happened to ya boy Travis?" I asked.

"Why? You want me to throw the oop for you?" She smirked.

"Fuck up outta here with that nut shit Simone. I don't want to have to fuck bul up again if he catch me at his crib uninvited," I responded.

"First of all, you know he don't live here so you fuck up outta here with *that* nut shit, Brett. Don't worry about him, okay? That's done. If you're talking about the picture in the living room...that day was very important. It's when I got custody of the twins..." She spoke in a certain tone that I learned about her. It meant she didn't mind talking about it but would rather not. I caught the hint and simply stated:

"Okay, my bad."

I never even knew she had to get custody. She always wanted all my truths but she had secrets of her own. I stayed quiet as she put her lasagna in the oven, poured herself some wine and asked me to come on the balcony with her. I sat down next to her as she rolled herself a fat blunt. She let me get my two puffs after awhile then she put it out.

"Brett, I fuck with you like crazy. I think about you all the time…I just cannot compromise my job. I'm finally doing what I always wanted to do and I just don't want to sneak around like Shayla and Trevor hoping I don't get caught. And you can't fuck with no bitches, point blank period." she said leaning back with her eyes closed.

"They sneaking around cause Shayla boyfriend does security. No but seriously. I ain't know you knew all the bad bitches," I laughed.

"I know everybody. That girl Maya? Gotta go. Oh, and ya little fake meetings with that fucking Chinese bitch…yeah don't look surprised you know who I'm talking 'bout, pussy. That shit gotta stop. At your cookout and on your birthday Maya wanna be all in my face. When me and Char out? Little Miss China rolling her eyes and shit. I'm really trying to be civil. Is y'all still fucking or what?" she asked irritated. I didn't know how she knew about the meeting with Neesha but I was caught and wasn't about to deny anything because them girls didn't mean anything. At least not like what Mone meant to me.

"She not Chinese, haha, she's Cambodian and Black," I said cracking up. Simone was so cute when she was mad.

"Nigga I don't care if she was black and blue! Don't play with me! I am five seconds away from letting Char dig in that bitch ass," she said fuming. Char was known as a fighter since way back, ha. I learned back in the day how she got down when my old gym used to hold matches with hers. She was known to knock niggas out for messing with her little cousins, too. I laughed at the memories. I didn't see it ever getting to that point but it was funny seeing how mad Simone was getting over bitches who didn't mean anything to me.

"Ard, ard. Chill baby girl. We just cool. I don't even speak to them girls, I really don't," I said grabbing her hand.

"Lying ass." She spat.

"I'm here with you 'cause this is where I want to be. That should tell you something, right?"

"Oh, you just know what to say, huh? Brett I'm serious I know you fucking bitches cause we not…Ya phone ringing every five seconds. We always gotta make a thousand stops when we together…You think you so lowkey but I always know. It's called intuition…why you look like you got caught with your hand in the cookie jar?" she laughed.

"I ain't feeling caught about shit…I just wanna know why you worried about bitches when you said we was just besties," I said making her get up and storm off. *Ain't nobody chasing bitches I'm selling* *dope baby...*After a while I got up to check on her. She was sitting in the middle of her black leather couch watching a movie. I sat on the end of the couch and pulled her close.

She wanted to cuddle and wrapped her arms around my waist.

"You smell good, boo," Mone said squeezing me.

I wore some oil I got from my old head Ahmad downtown, my gold chain, a fresh white tee and some gray sweat shorts. I started rubbing Mone's ass and got into this movie with KeKe Palmer that was made in Philly. It was a pretty good flick. Being alone with shorty was alright with me. I could get used to it. Shit felt good, you know?

Halfway through the movie she turned around to look up at me with her head on my lap. Just staring. Her eyes were slanted and I could tell she was feeling her wine. She propped her head up on the arm rest and pulled me in close for a kiss. Grabbing my hand, she guided me inside her shorts. I played with her clit and she let out a little moan. She was moaning while we kissed and was rubbing my ears. It was driving me crazy. I pulled her shorts off and picked her up. She wrapped her legs around my waist and pointed to her bedroom. I hesitated at first. We always joked about me finally getting some ass but now that it was here I had to stay calm and change baby girl life with the stroke! I was gripping her ass and kissing her slow and hard as we made our way in her room. Boss was growling which made us laugh.

Once in her room, I put her down and got undressed. She was naked by the time I turned around and I was stuck. She was looking too good laying there turning on some 90s rap music that came through the speakers hanging from her ceiling. Full breast, even copper skin from head to toe with that white toenail polish. She spread her legs wide open into a split with her finger in her mouth. She was just looking so open and ready for whatever.

I decided to leave my undershirt on. I had abs and all that but after getting hit I just wasn't as confidant with my shit anymore. Getting shot let me know I wasn't so invincible. Shorty ain't care though. She got on her knees on the bed pulling me close and pulled my beater so she could see my scars. She gently outlined the scars with kisses and took my undershirt all the way off, threw it on the floor, and whispered: "Eat it, King."

Listen we grown, you know what type time it was. I kilt it and didn't even hit yet. My beard was soaked and she scratched my cheek when she was cuming. She yelled out my name and started shaking all over. She ain't say nothing about a condom so I slid right in and had her legs pressed to her ears. Lil Mama was so tight I had to work myself inside. Once I was in it wasn't no stopping. She was scratching my back while she moaned and said she was falling for me. I slowed down and looked her in the eye.

She smiled and wrapped her hands around my neck and we got into this crazy rhythm. I picked her back up pressing her against the closet door and kissed her. She just stared at me with these eyes that made me give her this work you feel me! She was holding my neck so tight with her left hand and dug her nails in my back with her right hand. I grimaced at the pain but it was making me go harder.

I tossed her on the bed on her stomach and knowing what I wanted, she scooted to the edge and arched her back while she looked back at me smiling—her legs still shaking. I gripped her tiny waist pressing my thumbs in her back dimples and worked my way back inside. Dawg. I. Stroked. Her. Down. Mone's hair was laid out all wild as she moaned into the bed. I pulled out (thank God!) right before I came on her back and collapsed next to her. We laid there for a minute. We went for round two and after she got on top I was almost sleep. She laid her head on my chest, grabbed my hand and giggled.

"What's so funny," I asked wrapping my arm around her waist.

"So out of all the girls you really fuck with Ms. Simone, huh?" She grinned. I couldn't even say nothing, dog. Just rolled my eyes and smiled. She laughed and laid her head back down.

Yeah, Simone had me out here wide open.

We got up and ate some of her lasagna with some wine. I never had a woman cook for me besides my mom which meant a lot to me. Of course, the guys were telling me that they would be at the lounge that night. It was a Saturday so you already know that's where I was heading. While I was trying to respond back to the group chat, Mone slapped the phone down and dropped to her knees giving me the craziest sloppy I ever had in my life. Dog. In. My. Life. She would pull that stunt right before I left. Don't laugh but my legs felt like oodles and noodles. SMH. *She must want me to start acting crazy over her ass.*

"Brett can I trust you?" She asked after we were both dressed.

"As much as you can trust," I said standing by the door.

"Don't just tell me shit and have me thinking shit one way and it's not. Just keep it a stack. I'm a big girl and I can handle whatever."

"Stop worrying baby…Does this mean we can stop playing this game and you'll finally be my girl?"

"Hmmm…do you deserve it?" She giggled.

"I think I do," I said. I grabbed her by the waist and pulled her in for a hug, pressing my lips against her ear.

"I guess you can be my dude or whatever," she smiled showing her dimples, with her hands on her hips.

I kissed her on the forehead and told her I had to go. She had plans to kick it with her girls that night but was willing to flee them. I was feeling the same but money was to be made.

Once outside, I could see a tinted car parked a few houses down on the other side of the street. Nothing too strange but, I don't know. Something didn't feel right about it like a few days back at the Chateau. I had been lucky or better yet, blessed. Everybody from Unc, Brandon, D…down to the very last runner we had were locked up before. I never even got pulled over. Seeing that car was nothing out of the ordinary for a typical Saturday evening but I felt something in the pit of my gut knot up. How the hell would I keep these two worlds separate? I started my car, seen it was about 8:30 pm and sped off to meet with the gang.

AJ'S INTERLUDE

AJ was still trying to right the wrongs in his life. He did his dirt back in the day but he buried it in the hole he spent most of his younger years in. He felt like this was his second chance at a peaceful life. He wanted to squash one last beef he never reconciled over the years and that was with his old friend turned enemy Tesson McCoy.

They were boys as back in the day. Now? They were the last ones standing. Everyone else they ran with were dead or in jail. Tesson used to go by the name of Muscle back in the day. Now in days he just went by Tess. They sent flowers to a lot of mothers over the years. After AJ got locked up everybody—including his own brother—left him in jail alone. Olly made sure it was money and messages for him through their mother Susan before she passed but other than that, it was no contact. The next and last time AJ saw his little brother they were in a bar catching up on old times. AJ thought when he saw Olly he would shoot him for deserting him. Yet, when he saw him, he shed one loan tear and gave him a hug. AJ was in a halfway house and Olly was heading to New York with his family the next morning for a day trip with another failed artist. AJ wanted Olly to give the music up and focus on getting to the money again now that he was out of jail. He didn't shoot Olly's music dreams down like Olly did his plans of getting rich that night. AJ felt his anger all over again.

The brothers promised to get together that Sunday for dinner so AJ could see his nephews and then they parted ways. The next morning, he woke up to the daily newspaper stating that Oliver King—rumored drug kingpin—had been shot and killed while getting into his car at a gas station. It went unsolved and AJ felt bittersweet. No doubt he loved his brother but he was still angry about how Olly turned his back on him during his bid. He figured he would use his smart and fierce nephews to his advantage and get back on top as a way to ease his mind. When his old Tapatio cellmate, Ramirez, called him about a new business and a big profit, AJ had to take the opportunity. He was grooming his nephews for a time like this and everything was falling right into place. AJ knew he built a solid team with his boys and didn't need anyone getting in the way of what he started.

The one road block for him was the McCoy's. Tesson's brother, Spade, was in jail so things were calm. Spade was the thorn in AJ's side and with him now in jail thanks to an old friend, things were running smoothly. He faced new problems with the younger McCoy's because Tess and Spade's nephew, Flipp, was warring with Brandon and getting Brett caught up in the process. Jail messed Brandon up mentally and he wasn't thinking straight anymore but AJ still had Brett. With the McCoy's causing havoc eventually the Kings spot was going to blow up. To calm the streets down, AJ would offer Tesson a conversation with Ramirez. Split the city down the middle moving everyone else off the gameboard. A two-man monopoly. AJ felt they could reach more people that way. More customers—more money. Besides, he was getting older and tired of running. He was always paranoid death would come calling for him for past sins, but he would run from it for as long as he could.

Brett called his uncle and said Brandon was wildin' out and that Flipp was always in the middle of it. AJ just hated that it was another McCoy in the way and he surely couldn't have any young punk messing up his money. He needed to call a truce between himself and Tess so that the streets could continue to conduct business as usual. His political connects were also letting him know the streets were getting too wild and that he had better get a handle on it before they intervened…

Tess pulled up to the bar on 20th Street and Limekiln Pike and wondered why AJ wanted meet at such a place. They could have gone anywhere. This bar in particular brought back a lot of bad memories for him and he wasn't sure he could face those demons just yet. It had been fifteen years since Tess had a drink and he had been doing good. He owned bars around the city but all his staff knew he wasn't drinking and would make him special non-alcoholic drinks. Being at a bar from back in the day was a lot of pressure on the old kingpin but he was strong and couldn't back out now. The streets were drying up with Oliver's boys running things and he had to do something before the young guys in his crew switched sides. As he got out the car, Tess reached for his back. He knew his gun was there but it was a habit he developed over the years.

"Muscle Man," Tess heard his former acquaintance say.

"'Allen J ain't come to play' what's happening." The two old friends dapped each other up and Tess let AJ lead them in. He prayed for strength and took a seat at the bar.

AJ knew about Tess and his sickness. He decided to take advantage of it. This truce was real in the beginning but once some young girl told AJ about Tess' drinking, Allen couldn't help but to screw his enemy over one more time. AJ knew deep down calling a truce would only be temporary and killing Tess and Flipp wasn't the answer either. He had to sabotage them. AJ made sure his sexiest young girl was bartending this night in particular so Tess would feel the need to resort to his old ways. He tried to decline some drinks but the bartender looked too good to keep saying no. Tess knew his family and crew would be so disappointed in him but it would be his little secret. He asked for a shot and some ice and after some more convincing, had two rounds with AJ. By this point his demons started talking to him and he was asking for something a little stronger. While all this was happening, AJ was giving a very simplified version of what the deal would outline.

"Just talk to your young boys and I'll talk to mines. Less killing and more work. We'll meet up in a month with the boys to let them know what the plan is. We'll split the city right down the middle, you take the bottom and I'll take the top," AJ laughed. He was feeling his drink as well and whispered to the waitress to just give him soda and keep giving Tess whatever he wanted but to crush up a pill and mix it in. Peak was known to make people addicted and forgetful and that's exactly what AJ wanted.

"You still making moves huh! Man! Big Malc boys ain't no joke. A shame what happened to Olly. Oh Oliver. My brother…The hood mourned that day…" Tess slurred trying to grab his straw to down the last of his drink.

AJ began to pull out his wallet but Tess insisted that he pay.

"Man, I got this, you just go head and talk to your young boys and I'll talk to mines. To old times!" Tess said attempting to make a toast. He didn't realize he was left alone at the bar talking to himself. He thought AJ was still there the whole time. He knew he couldn't drive and decided to get some sleep in his car to knock the buzz off. Little did he know this was the beginning of a bad downward spiral.

FOURTEEN

One year later…October 2016…

Getting back in the game let me know how much I liked the perks of running an operation. It wasn't like when I was younger trying to earn my spot and get the bitches attention like Brandon. I was at the top giving all my guys a chance now. I gave them a way to feed they families. Buy they lady some nice shit. Give 'em a nice Christmas or my other brothers who's lay had to be crisp when Ramadan came around. Money and material things weren't the reason for it all but it felt good being on top when they were so used to being dirty youngbuls. Not by choice but by circumstance. Shit, some of them even enrolled into the local community college and trade schools. Dudes that couldn't imagine life outside of the 215 was thinking about being like me! Taking that money from the streets and flipping it into something positive. Judge us all you want but unless you or your folks were from the bottom you wouldn't understand. Niggas was tired of heating the house with the oven and eating oodles and noodles. They wanted to eat like kings!

"It was a cold winter when I stepped on the scene,
Mecca top, Reeboks, jumper's wit' gold buckles-the corduroys not the jeans,
walk around wit' a frown 'cause my swag so nasty,
everybody so worried I guess they always wanna pass me
but I'm ahead of my class I profess-call me Majesty
tell me why u really mad at me…
My lyrics gon' last
Beat me? Who me?
Now riddle me that
I'm-a get y'all kids leveled; get u poppin';
do something different like when Bey ain't tell us her album was droppin',
foot on the gas pedal wit' no breaks—we not stopping,
my dogs'll bite ya quick 'cause I'm on
kill ya in 24 for free 'cause my reach is too long

108

I win dog, I'm in dog, my words is too strong
like they popped up on pills
I am the realest, I am the illest
I ain't got nine lives so I aim to kill
click clack on your raps put the silencer on
Switch it up…B-Boy took me from
Section 8 and precincts to having Chinks in minks that's pink
Kill the cam—Paparazzi Lin said he got the links
To all your online accounts
We at our peak with the bounce…the fuck you think…
I am the last of the real, man it's crazy, you know? Surreal,
you'll never know how it feels 'til you're one of the last of the real…"

Shook laughed into the mic and said he needed a break. He was warming up with a freestyle that would go in "the vault" and the fellas were passing the blunt around. We were in a small studio down 10th and Market. Bo's little cousin Lin was finally in town and got us some free studio time. Lin started college in the city on that foreign exchange shit studying classical music.

About three weeks prior Lin just showed up at the D&K Lounge saying he was close with Bo and right away I knew who he was. Ever since then Lin was our guy. He was helping produce Shook's first EP. It was something big and we were working hard. Back in Beijing, Lin was producing for some local hip hop talent so you know I hopped on the chance to have him and Shook collaborate. Of course, we were maintaining business as usual with Peak. I gave in and let Shook and Lin sell for me. That way I was only touching the product during the initial drop at the stash house.

After we hit our first million, things with the guys changed. I did what I was good at and that was staying low and getting to the money. Ego's always got involved when money was around. Uncle AJ only met with us to make sure all the money was being accounted for and that the warehouse run went smooth. D was always around so things didn't change on that end. Brandon always felt a way about who was selling the most and was having bad mood swings so nobody wanted to be around him. Well except for Jay and Shawn. Jay was always looking for somewhere to squat and Shawn didn't have his own mind so they were Brandon's puppets.

I never had tension with the fellas before but I couldn't stop what I was doing to cater to them. While the guys were doing their own thing D, Shook and myself were working on building a music dynasty.

We had just left my old crib on Green Street where we always met to give my youngin's their re-up. Lin suggested we go to the studio so we could hear the new beats he was working on. Shook was always down to record something so me and D rode in my car and Lin rode with Shook.

I liked how Lin brought a different flavor to Shook's sound. He added symbols, old opera singers and adlibs to the music but still gave that raw street feel. We didn't care so much about structure. We just sat and vibed to the music. I wasn't a rapper but I had a good ear and always helped Shook with his flow and timing. He just had to get his content out and then he worried about flow. I wanted him to do those two things at once. He was still growing and learning and was eager to keep taking his style to the next level.

"It's like this. You all can say what I want to express. In my home we have to watch censorship. You have your free speech. I have not seen drugs done back home like in this city but I know what it is like to be poor and now have consistent money. We have something good here. Let's call it *Hot Soup*," Lin said messing around on the sound board. He turned his hat to the back and started fixing some drums he was adding. When he started bopping his head I knew we had something good.

"We bouta start some wavy unity shit. But Hot Soup? I don't know man," Shook said nodding his head to the beat.

"Is it not good?" Lin asked with an eyebrow raised.

"Where's the bitches? I need some inspiration if I'm gonna be talking about some damn soup," Shook said scrolling through his phone.

"We can get them later. It's only 8pm. We can hit up Brett and D's lounge after. Let's just finish this intro," Lin said trying to keep Shook focused.

Lin and Shook had become something like brothers since they were always around each other. Me and D were starting to see some returns on our investments and were planning a show to debut Shook's EP. Shook was bossing up and becoming his own man and I respected that. He could make money with me anytime. He wanted a piece of the pie and trusted me to show him how to make his own. I always dreamed of running a label and I was coming with something different. My youngin was feeling it and with the help of D's promotion and Lin's mixing, we were going to get the attention of eyes and ears everywhere.

"Yeah I'm with Shook on this one. Dina and the boys are gone for the weekend at her Mom's so you know I'm trying to have a good time," D said dancing in the corner.

"See that's why I always fucked with D. Let's get out of here," Shook added. We had only been there for a few hours but they were getting antsy.

"Brett please," Lin said not looking up.

"Look just finish the intro and we out in an hour or less. The faster you rap the faster we can go to the lounge. I gotta meet with Brandon anyway," I stated. Shook and D just rolled their eyes.

110

"Nah, lets hit the club and then come back to the stu." D suggested. The three continued to argue as I felt my phone vibrate.

Simone: Having fun Poppa?
Me: Yeah. You cool?
Simone: Good. Yes, I'm just chilling sipping wine and watching my shows.
Me: okay cool
Simone: Yeah. Baby how long are you going to be out? Me and Boss miss you.
Me: u know how it is, don't worry tho I'm gonna hit up the lounge to make sure shit cool for a little after the stu and then I'm all in ya face wit it
Simone: As long as I can sit on yours lol
Me: know that
Simone: Please be safe

***

Later that night, 11pm…D&K Lounge

"Yo lil bro, let's rap," Brandon said sitting down next to me.

"That bul Flipp is getting handled. His uncle Tess told him to chill out after Unc put some pressure on them clowns. Flipp feel like Tess getting old and soft so he came and robbed Shawn and Jay last night at the spot in Frankford. I was with Tina though. You know how I do it, though. I got the drop on his stash houses. I wanna have a word with him first tonight. If he ain't talking what I want to hear then we clearing that man out," he said smiling and rubbing on this shorty ass that found her way into our section.

"Okay but what you mean handled?" I asked. I ain't want no more bloodshed. Why not just keep the peace, get Shawn and Jay's shit back and keep it moving? The new wave of McCoy's was soft so getting the bread back wouldn't be an issue.

"Let's just say he won't be setting up no more hits. I'll take it light on him," he said as I passed him the blunt.

"What that nigga Shawn been up to anyway? He ain't been responding to the group chat," I questioned.

"If you just got robbed would you be in a talking mood?"

"I would've let the guys know," I replied.

"He told Unc and Unc told me to handle it," he said quickly.

"Ard…just don't do no stupid shit," I admonished.

"Haven't I had y'all backs this whole time? I know you don't fuck with Jay but Shawn is our guy. Like a little brother. Niggas rob my little brother? That nigga gotta feel it," he said turning red.

"Cool out hot boy," I laughed trying to change up the convo. I ain't feel like all that. Brandon could never just enjoy the moment we were in.

Shook and Jay weren't seeing eye to eye lately because of some unrelated family shit so they weren't really speaking. I stayed out of it because I really didn't care to know. I had no way to know Shawn and Jay got robbed. Shawn was laying low but I knew for a fact he would've said something. When we did our drop earlier that night no one mentioned anybody getting robbed. Shawn wasn't there to confirm anything but B wasn't the type to make shit up so I took his word. It was always fuck Jay but Shawn was our guy.

"So, you riding or what?" Brandon asked me.

"Man...okay, I'm in."

I still watched what I let Shook and Lin see so I had to figure out how to keep them fools busy. They were solid but still young and trigger happy. Sending them back to the studio wouldn't be too hard. I let Shook and Lin hold the keys to my new crib. I warned them not to break anything and not to invite more than 10 people. A penthouse suite for two 19-year-olds? Like giving Henny and crabs to a thot...

Nobody was dumb enough to go against this wave of the Kings—except for Flipp. He was just mad that the McCoy's didn't have the same pull as us. We had so many ties to so many small businesses throughout the city the Feds would be searching for years for any money if we were ever caught. Flipp could rob us on some run down on the spot type time—but they would never see where our millions were. I didn't see the need to go confront Flipp over, what? A couple hundred dollars? But Brandon was protecting his respect so I was down to ride. I let Simone know I was coming to her house after the studio but I didn't feel like letting her know about Flipp's, so I would just tell her we ran late.

"We bouta hit up the spot, see if ya homie D wanna come through. We gonna be in and out of there," Brandon whispered to me around 12...

We all got to the after hour that was in this rundown spot off 60th and Vine Street and I could feel the tension. Before I got shot you could catch me all over the city. After I got hit? I didn't do too much. I was just staying low key and only traveled to Germantown where Shook and his guys were. Niggas was always plotting and niggas knew who I was. This neighborhood in particular was McCoy territory and something just wasn't right in the air.

Soon as we walked in niggas wasn't so happy to see us but we stayed cool and spoke to some of the ladies in there.

"Wassup Brett Baby?" Uptown said grabbing me from behind.

"Hey wassup," I said gently pushing her off.

"What you doing up this way?" she slurred.

"You know...just been busy."

She looked like she popped a few pills or some shit. I never seen her like that before. Ma mentioned something about her being depressed but I hadn't seen her since the night I got hit at the lounge.

112

"Damn, I missed you" she said rubbing my arm. "I got just the girl for D too," Uptown smiled calling one of her homegirls over.

I had a few L's by this point and was willing to have some fun and she was just the girl for the party. Simone would kill me for giving her play but fuck it. I was out with the fellas.

Brandon sat at the small bar in another back room and talked to some chick that was sitting by herself while he waited for Flipp. I was glad they were in the back so if anything went down we wouldn't be seen.

Me and D followed Uptown and her friend with no name to the back in a room opposite Brandon with a rickety door. I guess Uptown got over her hate for me and just looked happy to have me to herself this night. She was so high off some pills she got from the McCoy's she was down for whatever. We talked while No Name rolled a chocolate dutch filled with sour. We all blew it down and after about 10 minutes Uptown and her homegirl got right down to business. Uptown was sucking my dick and No Name was letting D hit it from the back. I closed my eyes. Shit felt like old times!

"They some nasty little bitches," D said giving me a high five laughing. Soon as I came Uptown swallowed everything! Just then I heard voices raising and it sounded like the bar stools were falling.

"Fuck!" I yelled out. We could never just have a good time.

"Naw…I'm…coming nigga I be out there," D said smacking No Name's ass.

I pushed Uptown out the way and pulled D by his collar as he yelled out his number to the girls. This man never took anything serious. I ran out the room buckling my pants up with D following behind. I saw Brandon standing over some dude in the next room. Bul was on the ground pleading for Brandon to chill. Uptown came out behind us and once she registered what was happening she knew to grab her girls and go. A lot of other folks started leaving out too. I'm glad cause I knew it was about to get real.

"Nigga stop bitching! Say some shit like that again and I'll fucking kill. Pussy ass nigga!" Brandon shouted.

"Come on Bran. Put the gun down before—" I started to say.

"Brandon. Fuck is you doing? Got people running out of here. This my busiest night and you fucking up my paper! You in my hood, in my spot, fucking my bitches and threatening my niggas over some old shit? Over some community pussy? I'm thinking we bouta talk about some money. But you wanna talk about bitches? We all hit ya bitch and got her an abortion every other month until you got out. Haha! She been a hoe nigga," Flipp said getting a laugh out of his three stone-faced body guards standing behind him.

"How you get out so early anyway? Rumor has it you's a ratting ass nigga. You probably the reason a lot of my niggas got locked up. The sad part is ya nigga's is condoning that nut shit. Yo, get the fuck out of here, Brandon. You should be glad I even let you and ya bitches in here nigga. You really disrespecting me," Flipp said smiling and clapping his hands looking at me and D with every word. Just as fast as he got his words out, Brandon switched gears and aimed his piece at Flipp, shooting him in the head and chest.

BLAT! BLAT! BLAT! BLAT! BLAT!

Everything was moving in slow motion. Flipp's crew looked stunned as he laid there drowning in his own blood. Everybody else who was left in the front of the bar were now screaming and rushing the door. Brandon had one of the bartenders grabbing all the money out of the bar and putting it in a duffle bag. He had some other youngin's that were there roll up Flipp's body and head out the back. It was too orchestrated and everything was happening too fast. I knew this had been planned for a while. Flipp's security was shooting at us and we were shooting back trying to get the fuck out of there. I was pushing bitches out the way and everything.

"Meet up at Shawns," Brandon said as we all ran out.

Me and D hopped in my wheel and Brandon left with the bartender.

***

Uptown: that shit was crazy hope y'all cool. I heard somebody got shot! smh come through tho and my homegirl said bring that fat nigga D with u.

***

I drove around for a while before making my way to Shawn's spot. I had to make sure nobody was trailing me. When we walked inside, Shawn and Jay were counting the duffle bag money on the pool table. Once I saw Brandon, I snapped! I started fucking his old ass up! He was handling them jabs I was giving him though. Once Tess found out his nephew was dead, it would be an all-out war that I don't think Brandon was really ready for.

Niggas was joining the McCoy's after they started realizing we were getting money and weren't just letting anybody in our crew. It became them versus us. Flipp fed a lot of people and niggas would be ready to kill all of us if they knew their plug was dead. I was so mad I couldn't think. Brandon just fucked things up for all of us. Unc handled things and for once the hood was calm. With Flipp gone I knew the peace was gone too. I knew we shouldn't of went to Flipp's but it was too late for all that now.

Shawn and D broke the fight up (which was a few attempts of pulling me off bul) and Brandon was laughing on the couch, blood dripping down his chin.

"Nigga what the fuck is funny?!" I hollered.

"Shut up before somebody hear you!" Brandon shouted.

"Fuck you Brandon! You not even coherent right now. Popping pills, sipping mud and shooting at niggas whenever for

114

whatever! What you want niggas to go to jail because you got mad?" I demanded.

"*'You not even coherent right now'*, haha! Pussy, if you don't chill out," he laughed rubbing his jaw, "that nigga Flipp had that shit coming to him. He fucked my bitch and robbed us. That after hour was his biggest stash house and now we even. I told you it's handled nigga. I'm handling it. You ain't doing shit. You worried about ya bitch and that dumb ass music so much that ya head in the clouds. We running a drug business baby boy. Sometimes niggas gotta die," he said. I ain't like him playing my dreams or calling Mone a bitch. I started punching him again but Jay split us up. I fucked Jay up just cause.

"See you fighting ya own blood brothers over ya broad and niggas is out here handling business." Brandon continued.

"Did y'all niggas really get robbed? If so why y'all ain't handle it on ya own?" I demanded.

"How was we supposed to know how many niggas they had waiting for us outside? I...uh...I uh...just let Brandon know and then—" Shawn started, clearly high off pills.

"Shawn you fucking lying! Brandon said you let Unc know and that Unc told him to handle it! You can't even look me in the eye pussy! What the fuck is wrong with y'all niggas?"

"Chill out Brett you going hard like you sad Flipp dead or something. This the same nigga that was behind you getting shot," Jay chimed in rubbing his black eye.

"Fuck you Jay," I said getting in his face, making D get in between us.

At this point, I truly felt Brandon was just mad Tina was whoring when he got locked up and so now he wanted to kill every nigga she fucked. He would need an army because that was the whole tri-state! Brandon knew I wouldn't have came with him if he told me the real reason we were going. All this shit was dumb and our whole cover was about to get blown because these clowns didn't know how to solve shit quietly. Who kills a nigga over pussy? Pops always taught us to check the hoe not the pimp. This fool never listened.

"It's a way to handle things and that wasn't it!" I snapped.

"Shawn count the money and Jay get me some fucking ice," Brandon ordered.

"Oh, so now y'all Brandon's little bitches? This why y'all drinking mud all day and getting high off the damn product we selling? Do y'all realize what y'all just did or are y'all too high? Y'all niggas goofy as shit," I yelled.

"Chill out Brett ain't nobody going to jail. If you and D wasn't so hype to get ass and stuck to the plan we would've been in and out of there. If anybody snitch about tonight they a dead man," he said with a cold stare.

D was with the shits but kept his cool and stayed quiet. I could see on his face he was ready to shoot if I said shoot.

"I'll give it to you Brett you ain't waste a dime of Moms money from them boxing classes. You really used to be a faggot ass nigga. Haha. Go home and get some sleep. Lay low wit ya bitch til I hit you up. We gotta party more often little bro." Brandon said bumping into D as he turned the TV on and sat back on the couch. D was too quiet and I knew it was time to go before our terrible night got worse.

I dropped D off at Uptown's crib and told him get a ride home. He was pissed I wasn't coming through but it was already around 4:30am and I wasn't in the mood for that shit. I was cool off Uptown so I told him have a good time.

"Look baby boy…whatever you need let me know. I know that's your brother and all but we got a good thing going. I got the boys playing in the little leagues and shit. Dina getting alterations done on the house and her restaurant. You know what I mean? Things is going good for us…I'm just saying I got ya back, aight?" D said before getting out the car. I told him be safe, then made my way to Mone's crib.

FIFTEEN

By the time I got to Simone's it was 5 in the morning. I knew she would be pissed but I ain't give a fuck. I parked in the alley behind her crib and finished smoking a roach I had in the car. I put my windshield shade in the window, took my license plate off and put it in the trunk. I grabbed my gun, my duffel bag full of workout clothes I had in my car and headed up stairs. Boss growled at me as I walked in and locked up so I hurried into shorty room before he started barking.

I stripped down to my boxers, crawled in the bed and pulled Mone's naked body close to me. She was snoring lightly and I felt a sense of relief just being there with her. Flipp's eyes were going to be forever in my mind. They say a man that dies with his eyes open deserves it, but I couldn't help but to consider his family. His old lady was depending on him. Shit both his baby moms and six kids were too. He wasn't good but he was young. Just 29. My conscious was beginning to eat me up. I wasn't like Unc and Brandon. It was money over everything for them. I cherished life more. *Gotta leave this weed alone man, got me going...*

"Mm...what time is it, baby?" Simone whispered snuggling her head in my neck.

"It's late."

"I know that, silly," she said pulling my watch towards her. Once she saw the time she threw my wrist off her and faced me with her face all scrunched up.

"I'm yours all weekend. Just me and you."

"Why you ain't tell me you were going to Flipp's? They be shooting and shit up there..." she asked now fully awake.

"I'm here now." I said rubbing her butt.

"So how come you said you were about to leave the studio and come here, Brett? Why not just say that you got busy? Got me up waiting on you—I didn't even wrap my hair up, shit. You told me the

117

studio was a last-minute move. How many last-minute moves can you have?" she fussed.

"Long story baby, don't worry about it." *What the fuck man.*

"Brett don't be short with me," she said sounding frustrated.

Right then and there, looking at the street lights light up her face in her dark room, I wanted to tell her everything that happened. But one of the rules to this shit was keeping ya lady as far removed from BS as you possibly could.

"Listen Simone—" I started.

"Let me see ya phone," she said scrolling through hers.

"What?"

"Nigga let me see ya phone," she repeated with her hand out.

"What happened to trusting me?" I said sitting up.

"Cool." She pushed me away and threw her phone in my lap.

Apparently, Char's crazy ass was out trying to spy on Shook but instead saw me and the guys. Char sent Mone pictures of me and D walking to the back of Flipp's spot with Uptown holding my arm. Char was worse than the damn FBI!

"You got people following me now?" I asked.

"Fuck you Brett. I don't want no weekend with you. Just leave!" *C'mon Mone...*

"Babe I really don't need this right now and—"

"I don't need this either! This what I get for fucking with a youngbul! I asked you not to mess with her! I don't complain about your stupid cheating! I know what you be up to and I never complain, Poppa. Never! I just asked you to stay away from Maya! One bitch and you just can't. What. In. The. Fuck! Do this pill popping, smoked out bitch have over me that you just can't leave her alone with ya lying ass?!" she said throwing a punch.

"Look I blew it down with her and then she let D hit. That was it. She wit D right now. I'm here with you so what's the problem?" I said blocking her hits.

"Char said D was with some other girl! Lie again nigga!" she yelled mugging me.

"Char ass lying. Show me the other girl. Oh, wait. You can't cause it was only Uptown." *Aw, shit. Here we go.*

"Char is many things but a liar she is not. Wait...So...this bitch got a nickname? We giving bitches pet names?! I hate you Brett! Get the fuck out!" She yelled slapping me hard across the face. I gripped her up and gave her a shake. You would have thought I choked her out the way she started trying to get away from my grip.

"Man believe what you want to Mone," I said pulling her on my lap facing me. She was pushing me away but I had her gripped so tight she couldn't move.

Mone was crying and had her arms crossed but I wasn't paying that any mind. I was rubbing her back and sucking her tits so good that eventually she wrapped her arms around my neck. I pulled my boxers down and let her feel how stiff I was. She started kissing me crazy and lifted up just a bit so I could slide right in. I squeezed one of her breasts and lifted her up and down. I held onto her hips and lifted her up off the bed, and carried her out to the balcony. She was moaning, crying, and holding me as tight as she could.

"You really want to give this up..." She whispered in my ear.

"You ain't going nowhere," I grunted. She was scratching my arms up but I ain't pay that any attention. It was making me go harder.

I bent her over her couch she had out there, gripped her hair and pounded that thang 'til I came.

"Shit baby I'm fucking coming!" I grunted.

"Give it to me," she moaned through tears.

I bust all in her and collapsed on the couch. She crawled onto my lap shaking. We just sat there letting the early morning summer breeze cool us down. I never felt so connected to anybody in my life. Simone was the one. I had to get my shit together so I could move forward with her.

Back inside Simone crawled under the covers and told me to hold her as her body shook all over. So, I did. I held her until she was sound asleep. I had to get this shit with Brandon under control but at this point I couldn't trust anybody but D, Shook and Lin. Unc was MIA lately, and Jay and Shawn were loyal to Brandon so I couldn't fuck with them. I needed to talk to Eddy ASAP.

***

I woke up around 11 in the morning to Simone making breakfast in nothing but a pink silky robe, furry slippers and a sloppy bun. Shorty had beef bacon, banana nut pancakes, grits, eggs—all the good stuff! I hopped in the shower and tossed on some ball shorts and socks.

"Yo, ya bathroom got so much hair shit everywhere. I almost fell getting out the shower," I said looking through my email. I was responding to some business folks who decided to work with me on my plans for Germantown Avenue. They had a place on the block that needed to be fixed up and I had the bread to do it so I was working with them. I had D's construction team heading over that way that following Monday to get started. Things were finally coming to fruition with my vision of buying up the block.

"It's really not that bad in the bathroom," Simone laughed quietly. She still seemed upset but I didn't want to press.

"You cool, baby girl?" I asked as she slid a plate full of food in front of me.

"I'm chillin'," she responded. One thing I knew from being around my mom's family—a bunch of women—when they say they 'chilling' or 'cool' they not really chilling or cool. I knew not to say shit else.

119

We ate breakfast in an awkward silence. She asked if I wanted to blow one down with her afterwards so we went outside to the balcony.

"This apartment is way bigger than it looks. Are all the houses around here like that?" I asked.

"I'm not sure." She said blowing out smoke with her eyes shut.

"I might want to buy one and flip it if it's not already in good condition," I told her.

"You always on ya paper chase. I love it." She smiled.

"'Go get the money-go get the money'," I sang getting a small laugh out of her.

"Word on the street is Flipp died last night…" Simone said after about ten minutes of silence.

"Who you hear that from?" I asked.

"Brett…I know A LOT of people. I keep telling you this. Plus, I saw it on the news this morning that it was a shooting there last night. Brett what are you into?" She asked now looking me in the eyes.

Hell, if I knew. Shit started small and now it was bigger than I anticipated. Whenever Brandon was in the streets he made sure it was big. He ain't know shit about being discreet. I knew trouble was coming my way and I wished my Pops was alive to give me advice. I just stared at her quietly. I was wondering if she could really handle me and everything I came with.

"Look baby…My God-dad is a judge and his best friend's a lawyer. They'll do anything for me if I ask them to. I can help if you ever need help," she said.

I was hesitant. Shit the only thing I could think of was that she turned informant on me! A nigga was feeling paranoid.

"King…you don't think I know you in the game? I know who you are. We work together baby. I saw you clam up when Shay let us know about the Ramirez account. I was hype to see a brown man get rich, so, I did some digging and now I know he's up to something. Trevor couldn't have possibly known but something with Ramirez paperwork is off. Smells like money laundering to me…I didn't tell Shay yet 'cause I didn't want to raise any suspicions…" she said as calm and sincere as possible. She sensed my paranoia and talked me down.

"Didn't know you were being set up, huh?" she asked.

"What you want me to say Mone?" I asked with a blank stare.

"What are we Brett? We really together or we just having fun?"

"You already know I fuck with you, Mone."

"Yeah but what does that mean?" She said sitting on my lap. I wrapped my arms around her waist and looked her in the eye.

"You my girl, fuck you mean? You think I would be around like this if you ain't mean shit?"

"I'll take that…so do you trust me?" She asked holding my face in her little hands staring in my eyes. In that moment I knew I could trust her. Pops always said the eyes were the window to the soul.

"What you getting at Mone?"

"Your brother is fucking crazy and if we gonna be rocking out you need to know that I have your back. I got ya back at work at all times…let me have ya back when it really matters baby boy," she said calmly.

"Let's go inside and talk," I said getting up.

I didn't give myself up to Mone, shit I still had to protect myself, but I did let her know how I needed to get out of the game. I also let her know I didn't know how to explain all that to Unc. We also talked about how Unc was laying low for some reason. She assumed Brandon killed Flipp based on the news and what Char's nosey ass was probably telling her but I ain't touch on that.

"Mone, I'm trusting you. If you fuck me over…"

"King…baby. I promise you got me. My name and my word are all I have at the end of the day. Shit I have to watch my back too. Fucking with you ain't no easy thing. Bitches be hating and niggas be mad as shit because I be curving them for you…I'm really a down ass bitch, you'll see," she said standing up.

She stood in-between my legs and wrapped her arms around my neck, while rubbing my ears. She kissed my cheek and gave me a hug that I really needed. I didn't tell her that though—it was like she already knew. My life was getting crazy and knowing I had a shorty down to ride was a good feeling.

"I love you LL…and I got your back. I promise baby…I promise," she whispered in my ear as she rubbed my head. Bitches told me they loved me all the time but this was different. She wasn't looking for a response. She was just letting me know.

"I love you too Ms. Simone," I said squeezing her tighter to me. Damn I had it bad!

SIXTEEN

One month later...

"Okay so now that we locked the Ramirez account in, I'm projecting that we should be able to save close to $1.5 million in assets by the end of this fiscal year," I explained during the annual board meeting. With the help of Eddy, and Simone, I found out that I was really being set up to help Ramirez clean his money. Which meant Unc knew the whole time.

When I finally got a hold of Unc and let him know what was going on he didn't see the problem and made me swear not to tell my boss "or it's ya ass," he said with his gun out. I was guaranteed a commission but I had to make sure nothing got out. I was essentially working two jobs for bul. I was his hustler and his lookout. My hopes of getting out the game were getting further and further away and I was fucked up about the fact that I couldn't trust Unc.

"I love it Brett! This is why we hire young at New Enterprises. The freshness of the mind is something I wish I could put in a capsule and sell! Good work Brett," Jon said clapping.

"Not a problem, thank you Jon. Thanks everybody," I said taking in everyone's applauds.

"Mr. King? I'm Detective Pate and I need you to come with me. I have a few questions involving a shooting and murder," said a detective followed by two officers into the conference room. As they gripped me up, all I could do was stare at Mone. She looked completely shocked and everyone else looked confused. I had become the token black guy at my job and now, I was the stereotypical black guy.

"Whoa, whoa, whoa! Murder? Murdered who? I think you have the wrong guy buddy! If you just have questions why is he being handcuffed and who the hell let you in my office?" Jon demanded.

As they slammed me on the table to lock the chains on me, Ms. Mary came running in behind them and hysterically said "I tried to tell them they had to wait but they pushed me out the way."

So much time had gone by and the McCoy's hadn't retaliated. I figured they were planning something big for us but I wasn't sure when. They had to be smarter. It was like they were getting their ducks lined up so if they hit—they didn't miss. I believe this was a part of their plan. Smart on their part because everyone in the crew was getting paranoid. Even D, who was known to be everywhere, was moving real militant.

"Murder?" I repeated finally feeling the weight of what was being said.

"You damn right," the detective laughed.

"Jon this is a misunderstanding I promise you!" I yelled as they pushed me out the room.

"Yeah whatever man, you're going to jail and I'm gonna get my homies to fuck you up," the detective whispered in my ear smacking his lips. I felt violated and tried to move my head away making the cops push the cuffs harder into my back. I knew I had to remain calm.

***

"For some reason I don't believe you. I have a whole bunch of witnesses who say they saw you and your friend Delando at the after hour and one of you pulled the trigger and killed Nehemiah 'Flipp' McCoy. We found Flipp in a field rolled up in a carpet with bullet holes all in his body. Now all you have to do is tell me who did it. If you keep lying I can't help you Brett," Detective Pate said sliding me the pictures from the field they found Flipp in. Pate leaned back against the window in the interrogation room like it was checkmate already.

"Where's my lawyer at?" I asked.

"Your good buddy Delando is getting interrogated in the next room over," Pate continued. "Apparently he said you're the shooter. Now if he's telling the truth and he didn't pull that trigger you're going to go down for first degree murder. Conspiracy doesn't sound too bad either...Plus, I know what you're involved in so this will be a nice satisfying charge for me. So, who's the shooter, Brett?" he pressed.

"I thought you said you had so many witnesses. How come none of them can tell you who pulled the trigger?" I asked.

"Well for starters your own brother, uhh, Brandon King," he said reading off a paper in his folder, "is not trying to go back to jail because that would be his third strike and we all know what that means. He actually said that it was definitely one of you guys who got all mad 'cause Flipp came at your girl and came running from the back and pulled out a gun," he said feeling really confident.

"Nah Brandon wouldn't say no shit like that," I said getting more and more upset. One thing my Pop taught me before he died was to look a man dead in his eye and you could see if he was being truthful or not. This detective was full of shit. He knew some things but he didn't know the truth.

"So, tell me what happened? If you really didn't do anything why the secretive demeanor?" he asked leaning back smiling.

"I'm not saying anything else without my lawyer present," I stated calmly.

"What do you think this is? The movies? You don't just commit murder and ask for a lawyer!" Pate snapped.

"You have no proof and clearly your witnesses don't have good memory. So again, without my lawyer present..." I said folding my hands.

"Yeah...okay Brett. You're no Oliver King, that's for sure. Don't worry, I'm going to bury you under the jail and I'm going to fuck your bitch after that," he snapped walking out and slamming the door for extra noise.

"This clown must be new," I laughed at the window.

D wasn't no sucker ass nigga so I knew he wasn't talking no bullshit to get me himmed up.

After an hour my main man came busting through the door!

"Okay why am I down here now?" Attorney Womack said annoyed.

"Listen man it's a big misunderstanding. They trying to say I killed somebody that I didn't kill. Man, they arrested me in the middle of a work meeting!" I said now snapping.

"First things first—stop talking. Come on let's get you out of here." He said motioning for the door.

As I walked out the precinct I saw Dina and D arguing as they walked towards her car. That was my que to just keep going. Angry Dina was not somebody you wanted to be around.

***

"Well, this is easy. I can handle this. Your girlfriend says you were with her that night. By the way, she's so cute and then she opens her mouth. My God, she curses worse than my frat brothers," Womack said shaking his head as we sat in his home office. He was an old head who liked everything brown and leather. Bookshelves and globes filled his office and of course he had his vinyl's on deck.

"What she say, man?" I asked laughing at how Simone must have gone off on him.

"Let's just say I'm going to do everything in my power to get you out of the woods with this one, believe you me," he smiled sipping on some whiskey.

I explained everything to him. He was my mom's attorney and the only dude I trusted. I told him how it was really Brandon who did it but I didn't want to get him jammed up. I just needed this off of me.

"You keep protecting your brother and you're eventually going to pay the price for it. He's already being investigated for a domestic violence charge against his longtime girlfriend, Tina. To make matters worse, some girl by the name of, uhh, Trayanna is screaming rape. Now I don't—"

"Wait *rape?* Nah she a whore. She probably fucked, didn't get no money and now she mad," I said pissed off. I saw it too many times. I knew she was lying.

"Regardless, Mr. King, his bad behavior got you and your friend Delando locked up today for conspiracy and first-degree murder and all you're concerned about is not snitching and this Trayanna girl being a whore? By the way, as an experienced lawyer, even whores can be raped."

"So, you think he did it just because she filed a report? I heard she got fired, she probably looking for a come up," I snapped.

"Come now, Mr. King. As the son of *thee* Oliver King I take you to be a bit smarter than that. Brandon's bad is rubbing off on you if you can't tell," he said writing down some notes.

"What you think my Pops would've done?" I asked.

"He would've ceased all communication when advised to do so. Look, I'm begging you, for the love of God, no communication with Brandon. Please? Don't call him. Don't send anybody to look for him. Leave him be and let me do my job. You better be glad I have friends at the precinct because you would have been spending the night," he said motioning for the door.

"I was leaving anyway. I appreciate the help Mack!"

***

"You're done! You better be glad Jon and Shay convinced the board to let you keep your damn job because they were about to let ya ass go! I don't want to hear nothing about having to secure the damn bag or late nights or hanging at the lounge—none of that! You have a baby on the way and all you're concerned about is how fly your lawyer looked getting you out the damn interrogation room!" Simone yelled as I sat on my couch with my eyes closed.

"Mone, I really don't need this from you. Wait—*baby?*"

"No, I don't need this from *you!* They were going to keep you in there with no bail and all you can say is that you have to meet up with D tonight?! And yes, congrats I'm pregnant!" She hollered.

"A baby?" I asked still in shock.

"I'm a few weeks," she said now crying.

"A baby?"

"Yes pussy. What you not happy?" she said swinging at me.

"When were you going to tell me?" I asked as I let her light punches fall on my chest.

"I just found out last week and was trying to plan a special night for you," she said crying even harder.

I got up and started walking into the master bathroom where I took my watch and chain off, got undressed and hopped in the shower. Of course, she followed me.

"You better be glad I'm pregnant right now 'cause I would beat you the fuck up. Don't walk away from me when we're having a discussion!" She, shouted over the water.

"We're not having a discussion. You're yelling," I said calmly.

"I hate how nonchalant you're acting right now. I hate you!"

"I'm not being nonchalant, baby. Get in with me," I said sticking my head out the shower.

"Fuck you!" She yelled again.

"Well if this is what I have to deal with for nine months, I hope I have a son."

"I really can't stand you. You want a son for what? This drug shit is corny and you don't wanna stop. Like…What? You doing this forever? If we have a boy you gonna put him on too? You're about to be a whole father, got a badass bitch and still managed to keep a great job but you really can't put that shit down. You only doing this for you, man!" she screamed.

"I'M DOING THIS FOR US!" I hollered throwing the soap in the shower. I never yelled around or at her before. I knew it scared her. I heard her hiccup through her tears and start choking. I ran out the shower to make sure she was cool. She calmed down and stood there giggling.

"Well what's so fucking funny?" I asked upset that she was cracking up. All she could do was point to my limp soapy dick and laugh harder.

"Shrimpanese…wheeew. That's funny. Brett wash the soap off ya ass and take me to get some cookies on Main Street before you go see D, please," she said walking out the bathroom.

Damn, I thought to myself. Simone was having a baby! I was happy and then got paranoid all at the same time. A baby right now just wasn't a good idea…

SEVENTEEN

Summer of 2017...

It was a Friday night and a few months had passed since the DA started their investigation. Of course, it was dragging along. We were supposed to be coming to some type of outcome and I was just patiently waiting.

It was some crazy underlying beef with Brandon and me that Unc told us to dead. I didn't even know we were beefing! Against my lawyer's advice, I tried reaching out to bul but Brandon was holding onto a grudge like all of this wasn't his fault. His mind was all messed up from taking so many pills and drinking too much lean that no one could talk to him. Not even Ma.

Simone was 8 months pregnant by this point and was preparing for her baby shower the next day. I thought baby showers were supposed to be a surprise but Charmaine said the pregnancy was causing Mone to be super controlling. Char was more like her assistant during the whole thing. I was watching her make her little center pieces when she started complaining that she wanted water ice and $4 crabs from the seafood spot. That's all she ever wanted and I was tired of hearing about them. I didn't want to smell another crab but it was keeping her happy so I kept them coming.

"I want a half strawberry-half sour apple water ice and a cheese pretzel with my crabs too," Simone demanded.

We were at my crib and I was about to drop some money off to Uncle AJ down North. He called and said he was late paying the diner people and needed some help. Unc rarely asked me for anything, so it wasn't nothing to spot him I wasn't spending like I was used to with all the court stuff I had going on. Ma had a lot to say about it too. She basically cursed me out for lying to her and said she was done with me.

"I've did the best I could with you and your brother. No matter what I say y'all are gonna do what y'all are gonna do. Your father would be so disappointed in you Brett. If you get locked up or end up dead you remember that Ma tried her best with you. You wanna see ya mama cry that bad huh?" she sniffed into the phone two weeks prior. I really wasn't hearing what she had to say so we wasn't really speaking. I knew she was right but I had too much on my mind to worry about all that. Pops was dead and no matter what we did or said—Pops wasn't never coming back. I was in the streets trying to figure shit out and Ma ain't really get that. At least I didn't believe she did. I was still managing Shook but told him what my plans were concerning Peak and he gladly took over for me. I planned to stop by Unc's, drop off the cash, take the rest of the pills to Shook, get Mone's food and head back to the crib. That was it.

"I got you, baby. All that strawberry water ice you eating—that pussy better taste like strawberry," I laughed while rubbing her belly.

"You can taste it if you want," she grinned. She was so horny all the time I couldn't help but to laugh more as I slid my sneakers on.

"Hurry back, baby. Give me and baby girl a kiss," she said.

I squeezed Simone real tight while kissing her stomach. I stood up and gave her a slow kiss. I felt her belly jump and she randomly started crying.

"What's the matter now? I'll be right back, babe." I said.

"I just don't want you to go…I'm sorry I don't mean to cry. It just happens randomly, you know? Can I come with you? Please? We can go for a ride like old times," she begged hysterically.

"Now babe, you know I don't do no runs with you."

"But King—"

"No baby girl. I'll be right back," I assured her.

"You promise?" she was tearing up and held my hand tight.

"I promise. And I know—strawberry not watermelon." Then I left for the tire shop.

***

Unc: Change of plans. Meet me by the regional train. Allegheny.

I was a little confused because why would I be meeting him over there? Unc didn't usually text but he was hanging with some young girls so lately, I noticed, he was on his phone more and more. I just wanted to know why not meet at the tire shop like always. Why the train? I brushed it off and made my way.

I decided to turn off my air and rolled down the windows. I had been waiting for a while with no sign of Unc anywhere. I waited in the car under some trees across from the gas station. When I didn't see Unc's truck I knew something was up. I gave him a call. No answer. I texted Simone that Unc was playing and that I was about to get her water ice and head home.

That's when I felt a cold piece of metal knock me in my forehead.

I woke up tied to a chair surrounded by all these dudes in black masks in a dark and unfinished basement. I tried to talk but my mouth was taped up.

"Well, well, well…if it isn't the baby King. Should I kill you now? Or should I kill you later?" I heard a familiar voice say. I turned my head to see Tess staring me in my face. I didn't even realize Brandon was sitting next to me tied up as well. He was trying to mumble something to me but I couldn't make out what he was saying because his mouth was covered in blood and duct tape.

"Now your bitch ass brother told me your first body was Maj. Did you know that was my little cousin? Yeah, Maj was a McCoy. On his momma's side. My baby cousin. I asked Brandon did he know anything and after doing some digging for me he found out it was indeed you who killed him. Then a little birdy told me your brother here wanted to play tough guy by drugging and raping my niece!" Tess said growling. I looked down shaking my head remembering Womack said Trayanna was screaming rape. *That bitch!*

"Now, my nephew Flipp had one job. I gave him one simple task—kill the King brothers. Obviously, that was too big of a task for him," he said with his shoulders slumped.

"You know," Tess continued, "if I was you I wouldn't trust Brandon as a brother. He hates your guts. But as a worker? He's as loyal as a dog. Until he thinks in his demented head that you crossed him. Sorta like your dad and Uncle…Yeah, I knew Oliver. We went way back. The only real King out of the bunch. Not once did he kill anyone in my family. He always had his own mind. The good always have to die young, you know? Your Uncle is the one who told me he wished your dad was dead…Now, I'm not saying he killed him but what kind of twisted family hates their own flesh and blood? The McCoy's are too stand up for that. Ain't that right boys?"

"Yes sir!" the masked men shouted in unison.

"Oliver? Gone unfortunately. AJ? Under my fucking thumb since he threw you two boys to the wolves. That wolf being me. He owes me A LOT of money. He said he was out of the game and come to find out he's running a *multi-million-dollar* operation. You see, in this game if you make it out alive, you'd better stay out. So, he had two choices. Pay up the cash or pay up in blood for my nephew and baby cousin. He always loved money. Mama always said the love of money is the root of all evil. Allen literally gave me the idea to text you from his phone! Seems like a snake to me but Allen has always had snake like tendencies. He didn't get that from the real King family. Your grandfather Big Malc and my boy Olly would have never moved this way. But Allen's a Hill so who knows what his daddy's people get into. I digress. What was I even saying?" *Hill? Allen Hill? Unc isn't a King?* I thought to myself. *This nigga don't know shit. Once Unc finds out we tied up in a basement he gonna kill this motherfucker!*

"You was talking about how easy it was getting them niggas and—" One guy in a mask started to say.

"Negro I know what the fuck I'm talking about! Don't interrupt me! Now, yes, like I was saying—Brandon's high ass was easy to find even without AJ's help. But you Little Olly…you are the smart one. You have friends in high places and your sexy ass mama protects you. I had to think of a special way to get to you. You're like the invincible man. No matter what I did, I just couldn't get to you. Took me some months to orchestrate everything just right. But now…now I've got you. And you have a girl and a baby on the way…Anyway, AJ had a choice. You two or his money. I think you're catching my drift B-Boy. That's what the kids are calling you these days, right? Your Uncle is a very bad man. Trying to drug me and take over my shit. So now you and your brother are going to suffer!" he laughed.

"Who would like the honors?" Tess asked looking around.

Another man in a mask stepped up with a hard plastic bat.

CRACK!

One blow to the head and everything started getting blurry.

Lord, I prayed, *if you can get me out of this one I promise I'm done with the game. Just get me back home to Mone and the baby…*

BRETT'S INTERLUDE

*B*randon and all the fellas sat around in the pastor's study at David's Tabernacle. It was all thrown together pretty quick but I had the bread so I made it happen. Mom wasn't excited at first and told me not to rush things just because Simone was having a baby but I didn't care. I wanted Simone to be mines so I was going to marry her. Some folks were happy for us but a lot of people were upset about it. Everybody had something to say. Friends, or at least I thought they were. Simone's family…Ms. Mary protected Simone and her sisters with her life. It was cool to date her but marriage was another world. I guess she felt she had to protect her from me and all my drama. Even Mone's little sisters said she was moving too fast and that her career was just now on the rise. They told her that I was trapping her and to be careful. Why can't I just know what I want and go get it? Niggas kept a baby-mom or fiancé around for years. I'm right at mines and it's a problem. Just can't win I guess.

I blocked everybody out and focused on the mission. Me and Mone always talked about the future so I was being a man of my word. I had so much weight moving around the city on top of the money from my job so you know paying for a big and extra wedding wasn't a problem. We didn't ask nobody for shit and we were securing the bag. We were a power couple. All I needed to seal the deal was for her to be my wife. I ain't understand what everybody's problem was. Whenever you start doing well people want to hate because they don't understand that the elevation happened without their help. I kind of felt like Brandon was one of those people. He was the main one telling me not to get married.

"Dog, you sure you really want to do this?" he asked.

"Yeah man! I'm 100% sure about this chick! I'm on some Jagged Edge, Rev Run 'Let's Get Married' type time." I said brushing my hair with my hands and giving all my niggas dap. We were all looking at our champagne colored tuxes in the full-length mirror one more time. Me, D, Brandon, Lin, Shook and Shawn wasn't all seeing eye to eye with how the business in the streets was being handled, but at the end of the day we were boys. Simone and Ma had me and the guys looking sharp!

"I don't know man. Seems to me like you on turkey time. She seems like a gold digger," Shawn said.

"Pussy you wouldn't know a gold digger if she came at you with a bucket and a shovel, fuck out of here," Lin said making us laugh. Hanging around us hood dudes had his bidding game on another level!

"Nah, nah, nah. I agree baby brother," Brandon went on. *"She gets hired by your dumb ass at your job. Sounds like a stalker. Then she hops on ya dick when you got shot 'cause you were vulnerable. Makes sure she gets pregnant 'cause she know you young and pussy-whipped and then got you to wife her ass up. Sounds like a set up. What type of way is that to start a marriage?"* Brandon said staring at his phone laughing.

"Thanks for the words of encouragement B. Nah, nah, nah I really appreciate it," I said sarcastically. They were supposed to be my niggas and here they were trying to talk me out of walking down the aisle. I wasn't tryna be a player for life like these dudes.

"No problem. I hope that nigga Travis don't show up today, ha! He crazy man. Heard he kill niggas for fun when they take his women. You get her pregnant AND marrying her? You could be one of them niggas," Brandon said still laughing and fixing his bow tie in the mirror.

"He better not let this tux fool him then. I know we in church but Pops taught me to always stay strapped you feel me?" I replied.

"True that. Rest in peace to the big homie, ha. I know you fucked the bitch Maya again at ya bachelor party. You can't stay away from her man. I know Simone pregnant but just think about what we got going on," Brandon said.

"Y'all sound like a bunch of haters…You really dig this one huh?" D asked walking up to me, rubbing my head.

"Yeah. she the one dog." I said giving him dap making Brandon mad.

"Yeah well all we saying is be careful. Once a player—always a player. You gonna be a player for life," Brandon said laughing realizing him and Shawn was hating.

Just then Ma came in and kicked everybody out the room so that it was just me and her.

"Looking just like your daddy when he married me. Oh he would be so proud. You are truly a 'stand-up dude' as he would say. I miss that man…You sure you ready B-Boy?" Ma asked fixing my bow tie.

"Yeah Ma. She's the one. I'm nervous as hell but you know—I'm good." I said ducking a backhand.

"Stop cussing in the Lord's house." She giggled.

"I learned 'hell' from the Bible. 'Ass' too," I laughed.

"Yeah okay, boy. I'll beat yours you keep playing with me…I just wanted to check on you and tell you how happy I am that you're settling down. I'm getting older and it's nice to see you doing so well for yourself," she said now tearing up.

"Thanks Ma," I replied hugging her.

"As much as I didn't like Simone at first, I can say, knowing her mother isn't around just drew her to my heart. She's a beautiful soul. I don't have any girls, so for her to allow me to help plan this day means a lot. I must say she makes a

*beautiful bride. Pregnant and all," she said smiling. Mom wasn't too happy when
she had to keep getting the dress altered after finding out Simone was pregnant.*

"I appreciate that Ma. She talks about you all the time. I'm glad you
gave her another chance," I smiled.

"You ready, B?" She asked.

"Yes ma'am."

"Let's go get 'em," she winked.

***

"Wake up pussy!" a voice yelled throwing water on me. The
voice slid a bowl of chicken broth and a straw in front of me on the
floor. I jerked around and realized I was just dreaming. The only way I
could tell the difference from night and day was the little light that
would peak through the basement window when the sun was out. My
ankles and wrist were so sore from being tied up. *Two weeks,* I thought
to myself. I laid my head back down and thanked God no rats were
running around the basement or sniffing me like the last couple of
days.

"How does it feel to spend ya days in the hole, pussy boy?"
The voice laughed.

"This nigga never did a day in jail. I'm sure he wished he was
anywhere else but here," the second voice said. The second voice
sounded familiar but I just figured I was tripping.

"Better drink up dickhead. If you start dying down this bitch
we gonna let the rats finish ya off." The first voice chuckled.

"Why don't we just kill this nigga already? Shit Brandon dead
now so what Tess waiting on? He doing too much. His brother Spade
would have offed these niggas and been done with it. I need him out
my basement, man" The second voice said again. My eyes grew wide as
I looked back at the crack in the window. *I knew I wasn't tripping. It's that
nigga Jeff! I'm across the street from Shook and Ms. Jones.*

"Kill him for what?" the first voice continued. "It's better
while he alive. He worth a lot of bread. Tess tryna get his bitch to give
up the ransom money but her sexy ass a gangsta' forreal and she ain't
budging dog. Plus, you know he don't really wanna kill bul. Tess and
his pops was cool back in the day. Tess just on that shit now so this
like a game for him. I knew Brandon ain't have a chance after that shit
with Trayanna hoe ass, though. Hate it had to be him..." they
continued walking up the steps away from the basement closing the
door again. *Niggas talk too much. Wait 'til I'm out of here.*

I didn't want to lose my strength so I drank the broth and
prayed they didn't poison me. I shed a tear for my brother but couldn't
dwell on it. I had to keep my mind from slipping away. I laid my head
back down on the cold concrete floor and dozed off again to my dream
of me and Simone...

134

EXCERPT FROM
THE LAST OF THE REAL SERIES
PRESENTS:
KEYSHAWN McCOY
(BOOK TWO)

Prologue

Sometimes when I think about my childhood, it amazes me that I survived that shit. Like, I am still walking, talking, and breathing. People really let life break they asses…but not me. I guess being a McCoy just made me hate that type of person. The "what does it matter" type of person. I mean, I guess it's also human nature to cope by any means necessary. Or is it?

The first time I was held at gunpoint I was six years old. I guess that's why when it happened to me this night in particular—I didn't panic. I didn't cry or shake uncontrollably like I did when I was a little girl. I just stood there. I prayed my daughter stayed asleep in the next room and just did what the fake shooters told me to do.

Everything they were talking about was foreign to me but I tried my best to appease them. If it was just me? Shit would've gone down differently. I would have grabbed my gun out the cabinet as soon as I heard the front door open…but…all I could think about was my baby girl sleeping soundly in her re-decorated room. Princess Tiana everything of course, even though I hated the color green. I mean, unless we were talking about money…

Anyway, for some reason, I couldn't get my feet to move. That was the only part that was pissing me off. I couldn't move because of who my fake shooter was. The reason my life didn't flash before my eyes when I felt the cold metal on the back of my neck was because I felt sympathy. Something I tried hard to stay away from. Here they were, breaking and entering and *I* felt bad. I knew in my gut who they were. Well at least one of them but I knew they weren't going to kill me. They just wanted to scare me and honestly, they had good reason.

Poppa Spade always taught me to show no fear, so I didn't. I could smell the fear on Brett's baby-mom though. Not the kind of fear that I should've been feeling being held at gunpoint…She had a fear that only a mother could understand. It was the fear for her unborn. I

137

mean, how could I blame her, you know? My family would more than likely disown me but I was more than willing to help. My Uncle Tess was a bad man and I wanted the nigga dead. I guess you can say it would be a win-win for everybody involved. I said a silent prayer and slowly—with my hands held up in the "don't shoot" position—turned to face the two women who were trying to decide my fate.

"Where is Brett?" Simone asked sternly.

"I don't know, sweetheart. But I believe I can help you find him. Only if you want me to though," I offered.

"Why should we trust you?" her accomplice questioned. It took me a while to place the voice but then it came to me.

"Char? So, you're definitely Simone," I blurted out.

"You know this bitch like that?" Simone fussed.

"Listen, you said figure out who would know something so I did. Did you have anybody else in mind, heifer?" Char said with her hands on her hips.

"I smell crabs. You was eating crabs?" Simone asked.

"Uh, yes. From Bob's actually. You want some?" I asked.

"You damn right. Welp, cat's out the bag. Now I can take this hot ass mask off. Here Char, hold the gun. I'm fucking hungry," Simone said duckwalking to my fridge. *This bitch making herself real comfy, I remember them prego days...*

"Ooo she got shrimp too. You want some Char?" she asked sitting on my lounge chair.

"No, I don't want no shrimp. Well, it is from Bob's. Just save me some." Char said glancing over at the tray Simone was holding.

"Uh, could you eat it at the breakfast bar?" I asked politely.

"Fuck you and fuck ya breakfast bar." Simone said moving around in the chair to get more comfortable.

"So...you say you can help me out huh?" Simone asked cracking open a blue-shelled crab and pulling all the meat out like a pro. *Why would I give her my crabs? Oh my gosh! She's getting garlic sauce all over my white rug!*

"Yes...I believe I can help. You guys would have to give me some time to put a plan together. I know my uncle. Tess wouldn't kill Brett. He loves him 'cause of who his dad was. But I do know Tess loves money and will do anything for it. Like what he's doing now. If he does have Brett tied up somewhere like y'all are saying, it's only to get Mr. AJ or Brett's mom to give up some money." I said calmly.

"But why my man?" Simone said now crying and choking on my dinner. Next thing you know she was throwing up all over my hand-knotted white Persian rug! That shit was custom made!

"Bitch are you serious?!" I yelled, forgetting Ameenah was sleeping in the next room.

"Oh shut the fuck up and stay still before we take ya baby for ransom, bitch," Char said cocking the gun. *Stay calm Key Baby. Char a thorough bitch but she ain't gonna shoot you. Or will she?*